CONT

	Content Warnings	v
1.	Willow	1
2.	Mason	12
3.	Willow	29
4.	Mason	40
5.	Willow	53
6.	Mason	62
7.	Willow	79
8.	Mason	87
9.	Willow	97
10.	Mason	107
	About the Author	115
	Also by Jade Swallow	117

HIS MILKY ADDICTION

JADE SWALLOW

Copyright © 2025 by Jade Swallow

All rights reserved.

No part of this book may be reproduced in any form or by any electronic or mechanical means, including information storage and retrieval systems, without written permission from the author, except for the use of brief quotations in a book review.

CONTENT WARNINGS

This book contains a forbidden erotic relationship between two consenting adults and is intended for readers over 18. That being said, this book appeals to very specific tastes, and some of the content mentioned may be triggering.

A non-exhaustive list of content includes: A taboo relationship between to-be step siblings, lactation kink with loads of filthy milking, a hucow heroine, breeding kink (unprotected sex), oral sex, dirty talking, pregnancy, pregnant sex (with a baby bump), steamy scenes in public, and typos and grammatical errors.

Please note this is a work of fiction featuring imaginary scenarios. Only read if you are comfortable with the above themes. The author does not endorse the beliefs or actions of the characters.

If you read this book anywhere other than Amazon, you have an illegal pirated copy. I encourage you to research the harmful effects of piracy on authors and obtain a legal copy instead. Thanks.

1

WILLOW

Few things make my heart flutter as much as Mason Astor does.

The hottest guy in Astor High walks in, his cerulean eyes casting a spell on my body. I can't take my eyes off him, and I'm not the only one. He's followed by a group of adoring girls wherever he goes. I hear the high-pitched sounds as he strolls by casually, a hand in his pocket.

"Congratulations on turning eighteen, Mason. I wish I could attend your party." One of the cheerleaders speaks up. I don't miss the push-up bra Alanna is wearing, thrusting her tits up to her face. Her miniskirt reveals most of her legs and it's no mystery that she's trying to seduce him.

"Thanks. It was just family," Mason replies politely. He looks like a Hollywood star with that dreamy, dimpled smile, a straight nose, and that jaw that's chiseled to perfection.

My heart begins beating faster as he gets closer to me. I feel my nipples tighten under my school uniform, and if it weren't for the padded bra I was wearing, he'd know how hot I am for him. I've had a crush on Mason for ages since we did a Chemistry project together. I always thought he'd be stuck up and self-obsessed, but he was surprisingly kind. That just worsened my unrequited love for him, because I know rich guys like Mason don't end up with scholarship students like me.

"Maybe next time?" Another cheerleader barges in, fluttering her eyelashes at him. Mason, however, remains unperturbed by her actions. He carries himself with confidence, replying to her with a lopsided smile.

Mason Astor screams 'old money' and it's part of his appeal. His family is an illustrious business family that owns the school. His dad and mom got divorced when he was a kid, but he's the most pampered child in the family. The teachers adore him and nobody dares to go against his word. As a scholarship student who got in on her own merit, I'm supposed to hate him. Except, he's way too nice to hate. Mason has a heart of gold to go along with his golden spoon. He's never abused his power as an Astor and shows up to classes on time. He studies hard, and he even got early admission to Harvard. He's a true example of nobility, someone who spends his weekends doing volunteer work.

I instantly shrink away as he approaches me, my back pressing on my locker. He smiles at me, his dimples lighting up my day.

"Hey, Willow." My heart threads to burst out of my chest when he pauses in front of me. This might be the best thing that's happened to me today. I clutch my books closer to my breasts, hiding the secret I've been keeping from everyone. I can already feel the milk exert pressure inside my breasts and I know I'm so close to leaking. I screw my eyes shut, wishing to be spared that embarrassment. I started lactating a few days ago and I don't even know why. I'm a virgin so I'm pretty sure I'm not pregnant. Maybe I should get myself checked, but I'm too afraid to tell Mom. She's been busy these days, preparing for her wedding with Hugh. He's mom's new boyfriend and I've met him twice. He proposed to her last weekend and she's been over the moon ever since. All I know about Hugh is that he's rich and seven years older than my mom. It doesn't help matters that we're supposed to move in with him this weekend to prepare for his life with Mom as a couple.

"Hey…." I inhale deeply, feeling my nipples tighten. The familiar tingling in my teats begins, my pussy throbbing as I inhale his spicy, woody cologne. Mason is like the sun and I feel pale and insignificant compared to his bright personality. When my books brush against my tender nipple I moan involuntarily, the pain radiating around my breasts. I bite down on my lower lip awkwardly, noticing Mason's eyes fixed on me. They darken when they slip to my lips, lingering there for a moment before turning to my inflated breasts squeezed by my books. I clear my throat, trying to regain a semblance of dignity. "Good morning."

Before Mason can reply, the school bell rings, jolting me out of my reverie. With an awkward smile, I run away, feeling my tits throb with every bounce. Mason remains staring at me, frozen in place as I round the corner and slip into the classroom. Oh my god, why am I so awkward around him?

Taking my seat at the back of the room, I pull out my phone. I gaze down at the link to a location that my mom has sent me and sigh.

It's moving day today.

Mom's been excited to move in with her fiancé ever

since he proposed. She kept talking about how grand the proposal was. Apparently, he booked out the swankiest restaurant in town and got it decorated with roses just for her. Hugh proposed to her with a massive solitaire diamond ring and Mom accepted right away. They've only been dating for three months, and it makes me wonder how serious she is.

Mom has a thing for rich men and though I'm happy for her, I can't help but wonder if she's marrying Hugh for his money. My mom got pregnant when she was in high school and soon after, my dad left her. She didn't get to go to college but got her high school GED and started working as a secretary right away. Raising a kid as a teenager wasn't easy and she struggled to make ends meet by taking up odd jobs. Her family disowned her so, she was on her own. I love my mom and respect everything she did to raise me, but I can't help but think she's rushing into this marriage. After she heard I got into Harvard, she was determined to find a way to pay for my tuition. Though I got a scholarship, the living expenses are too much for mom to handle on her current salary.

Mom: Come here after school. Hugh wants to introduce you to his family.

I haven't spoken much to Hugh, but I know that he has a son from his first marriage. I have no idea how old his son is, but I'm kinda excited to meet my stepbrother.

Me: Sure.

I instantly become aware of the warm, tall body that fills the seat next to mine. My eyes look up from the phone to find Mason staring back at me. Instantly, I drop the phone and gawk. What's he doing here? Doesn't he always sit at the front?

"Good morning, class." The English teacher, Mr. Trent,

bursts in with a smile. I don't know how he manages to be cheerful all the time when I'm constantly drowning in teenage angst.

"You were distracted this morning," he says. "Are you okay?" His gaze slips lower to my new, bigger tits that are bursting out of the white shirt of my school uniform. The button holding my chest together hangs by a thread. No wonder I feel so tender and sore. I'm engorged.

"Oh my gosh!" I stand up, horrified. It's been a while since I pumped. In my rush to get to school in time this morning, I forgot to milk myself this morning. I have no idea why they fill up with milk, but I've been doing some research online and it says a hormonal issue can trigger sudden lactation. Maybe I really need to see a doctor about it. I've been considering getting a breast pump but I don't want mom to be suspicious. She's always discouraged me from interacting with boys, worried I'd get pregnant at school like her. If she finds out I'm lactating, she'll think I'm pregnant.

"Willow." Mr. Trent brightens up. "I didn't know you'd be so enthusiastic about the Shakespeare group project. Why don't we start with you?"

"What?" My skirt almost grazes my knee, but I feel exposed. I am moist between my legs and I know it. From the way Mason looks up at me, he does too. I try to hold my breath to prevent my shirt from popping open but it's a struggle when I feel something wet around my breasts. Oh god, I'm leaking. My mind goes crazy, trying to find excuses to escape the classroom, but with every moment I stand there, more and more milk trickles out of my swollen teats until I can feel my bra getting wet.

"You'll work in pairs for this project. Each pair will be assigned a sonnet by Shakespeare to analyze." I can't hear the rest of his sentence. Panic grips me and I look around for a way to flee. I need to get to the bathroom fast.

"Let's work together." Mason stands up, putting his coat around me. I don't miss the way everyone's eyes turn to me, some of the girls glaring.

"Huh?"

"You want to pair up with Willow for the project?" the teacher turns to Mason, surprised. I'm not part of Mason's social circle. He is friends with other rich kids and just the fact that he's sitting next to me instead of them is weird. As a scholarship student, I am mostly on my own. When I managed to get into the prestigious Astor High on a scholarship three years ago, Mom was ecstatic. She thought it'd improve my future prospects, so I took it up. However, it soon became clear that I wasn't like the rest of them. My classmates had private jets and went to Paris for weekend shopping trips while I stayed in a one-bedroom apartment and studied my Friday nights away. Though they weren't obviously rude or impolite to me, I could always feel the difference in our stations. Over time, I just took to eating alone and spending most of my time in the library.

"She's got all As. I can't go wrong with her." Mason shrugs, deploying his charming smile. I gaze down noticing a wet patch on my breast. Mason pulls his coat over my shirt, trying to hide it. When I gaze up at him, he smiles and I have no defenses against that smile. He's trying to protect me. My heart melts at the kind gesture.

I sit back down as the others pair up. I turn to Mason, knowing I'm being watched. He doesn't mention my wet shirt, but I know it's growing damper by the moment and soon, even his blazer won't be able to cover me. My cheeks are hot pink when I meet his eyes. "You...didn't have to do that," I tell him. "I know you wanted to pair up with Shane."

Shane is Mason's best friend but he's not at school today. He comes from a rich family too, but unlike Mason, he likes to take advantage of his royalty status. Shane spends a lot of his time out clubbing and partying and he's often absent from school.

"Shane isn't here today," Mason says. "Besides, I need some brains in my team."

I smile. "Says the honors student."

I find myself opening up to his bright, warm personality right away. Mason has confidence but he's not cocky, which makes him such a rare breed.

"It never hurts to have two brains working together. Besides, if I pair up with Shane, I'll end up doing all the work."

"I thought you had tutors to do it for you," I pause, realizing I voiced what was in my mind and gasp. "I'm sorry....I didn't mean it like that."

"It's okay." He brushes it away with a wave of his hand. "I liked working with you on the Chemistry project. We got an A, remember?"

I nod. I was a nervous wreck throughout the project, working extra hard to prove that I could match up to Mason. We barely spoke, even though he was always trying to organize meetings with me. I was too self-conscious to dare to speak to the Mason Astor. The girls always glared at me whenever we sat together, making it known that I wasn't good enough for him.

The rest of the class pairs up and Mr. Trent announces, "Okay, now that we're done making pairs, let me remind you that this is the final English project you'll do before you graduate. I feel a little sentimental knowing all of you will be gone in a few months." Someone on the front row snorts. "But I hope you'll do your best and make it something to remember."

I swallow. I'm turning eighteen next week and in three months, I'll be done with high school. I am looking forward to going to college. With my mom marrying Hugh, my expenses will be taken care of. Though I love learning, going to Astor High has been a tense experience. I can't wait to graduate. I turn to my left, studying Mason's profile. He might be the only thing I miss about Astor High.

I feel something wet drip onto my thigh and look down to notice that my shirt is soaked. The room fills with the scent of sweet, nutty breast milk, catching the attention of a few people who turn back.

"What's that weird scent? Can you smell it?" Instantly, my spine straightens. My shirt is wetter than before. It's turned translucent and my red bra is clearly visible under it. I gasp and Mason's head turns. Before I can do anything, he grabs me by the arm and stands up. Mr. Trent turns to him, an eyebrow cocked up.

"We're going to the library to get started," he says, dragging me away from my chair. I can't help but follow his lead, pliant like a rag doll. It's so embarrassing that I can't even wiggle myself out of such a situation.

"Mason—"

He's never walked out of class before, maintaining his image of a good student. I feel so bad that he's breaking the rules because of me. Mason drags me out of the classroom and nobody speaks a word because his family owns the school. I follow him wordlessly, feeling the ache in my breasts intensify.

"Mason," I call out his name as we near the girls' restroom. He comes to a stop, reaching for the handle of the restroom and pushing us both in. I let out a scream, worried the other girls might see us together, but there was nobody in there. Mason opens all the stalls to check if the restroom is empty and after confirming it is, he pushes me against the door.

I moan as my tits bounce, leaking more milk. His blue eyes are blazing with hunger as his coat falls off my shoulder, revealing my wet shirt. There's no salvaging it. My red bra is clearly visible under the fabric. Mason's eyes widen as he takes in my huge, wet tits, licking his lips.

I hear a pop and the one button that was hanging on for its life clears away, offering him a peak of my cleavage. I breathe silently as Mason gazes at my exposed throat. The first three buttons of my shirt are off and there's no hiding my rack. He lifts his finger, gently brushing the space between my breasts. I moan when he touches me there, heat pooling between my legs. My thighs rub together, but it's no good. I want him touching my wet pussy, feeling how I leak for him.

"Why are you suddenly so wet?" he asks. His finger swipes over my bare skin, lapping up my titty milk as I struggle to breathe. He's so close, touching me so intimately and my body wants more. I want him to take off that sodden shirt and touch my aching nipples with those sturdy fingers. Every brush of his skin against mine is delicious. "Is that...." He brings his wet, cream-coated thumb to his mouth and licks. "Milk?" His head snaps up. "Are you pregnant?"

"No!" I panic. "It's just...I need to see a doctor. I don't know why I'm lactating all of a sudden."

It feels weird talking about producing milk with Mason, but damn, if it doesn't make my body glow like a firework.

"Lactating." He tries the word on his tongue. "I thought only pregnant women lactate."

"Not always," I tell him. "I don't know what's going on with my body but I assure you, I'm not pregnant."

He backs off a little, but he's still touching me. "So, your tits fill up with milk every few hours?" He tries to recall what he knows about lactation and I find it endearing that he's trying to understand me. But him saying 'tits' might be my new secret fantasy.

I nod. "I'm sorry you got dragged into it. I meant to tell my mom but...things are busy at home. I'll figure it out."

I feel I've unlocked a new level of intimacy with Mason now that he knows about my lactation problem. Nobody in the world knows I'm producing milk except me.

"That's why your breasts get so big, huh."

He noticed. "Yeah. I know it's weird."

"No." His voice is a deep whisper. His finger explores my breasts again and I don't want him to stop. I lean into his touch, pressing my soft, pillowy breasts against his palm. He grunts low and I close my eyes, letting him draw wet patterns on the tops of my breasts with his index finger. I'm soaked through, but I don't even care. All I want is to feel Mason's hand touching my aching breasts and letting me know he's nearby. "It's pretty sexy, actually."

"I...Thanks." I whisper, a little disappointed when he stops touching me. His fingers come away, putting distance between us. "I'm so sorry you had to cut class because of me." I snap my eyes open, still struggling to fight his gravity.

He leans closer, cutting off my words with a finger to my lips. My heart races as he drags his thick, masculine finger over my lips, cupping my jaw. His thumb brushes my lower lip and I inhale sharply, feeling my pussy clench in response. Mason turns me on with every touch.

"You're so beautiful when you blush." His voice is huskier than usual. I can see the desire darkening his eyes. I feel how much he needs me. If he dipped his head and kissed me right now, I'd just let him. His thumb grazes my lower lip and the air crackles with tension. My body wants him to take control, to press me against that wall and have his way with me. I close my eyes when he brings his lips a little closer. Every breath burns my lungs as I wait for our mouths to meet. Just when I feel the feather-light touch of his lips against mine, the bell rings.

Trrrrrrrr.

The loud sound pops my fever dream and Mason backs away, raking his hand through his dark blond hair.

"I'm sorry." I come off the door and he reaches for the handle, opening it. "See you around."

Then, he leaves, my chest aching not just from the buildup of milk, but a longing for the one man I can never have.

It's official. I'm totally in love with Mason Astor.

2

MASON

I'm in a weird mood when I get home. My body is thrumming with the awareness of what I did in the girls' restroom today. I can't believe I almost kissed Willow. If I'd taken just one more step toward her, she'd have felt how hard I was for her. She looked so damn sexy with that shirt open, those massive milky tits begging me to suck on them. And I swear to god that if that school bell hadn't rung, I'd have milked her dry until I could feel that sweet, nutty titty cream coating the insides of my mouth.

I've had a thing for her ever since we did that Chemistry project together. Willow is so shy and quiet, hiding behind her books, but she's really smart. She prefers to stay alone because she thinks the other rich kids won't be interested in her, but I find myself captivated by her mysterious aura. She's hard-working and so cute when she blushes. I can't take my eyes off her whenever she's close and I'm slowly going crazy. I need to tell her how I feel soon.

My Rolls Royce pulls up in the circular driveway, and I notice a U-Haul parked right there.

"Your new stepmother is moving in today," the driver,

Harold, reminds me. He's been working for our family for over four decades and he's someone I trust.

I'd almost forgotten that Dad's latest fascination is moving in with us. "She's not my stepmother yet." But we both know she will be. Dad already proposed to her.

Dad's been dating Jennifer for a few months now. She had lunch with us once, but I never really took to her. There's something predatory about her like she's interested in Dad only for his money. When he told me he was marrying her, I tried to stop him. I went to Mom's for a week, but Dad didn't change his mind. My parents got divorced when I was six, and my mom moved away. Though I've stayed in touch with her, I grew up in the Astor mansion because my dad is the eldest Astor son. Someday, this empire will pass down to me. I've been prepared to take over the business since I was young.

With my bag in my hand, I get off to find my future stepmom walking out of the front door. Her blonde hair pulled up in a ponytail, her face caked with makeup, she smiles at me.

"Mason." Jennifer waves at me, dressed in a yellow sheath dress that probably cost more than her monthly wages. I find it irritating how she's always trying to look elegant like she's trying to convince everyone that she belongs in our world. She's a social climber and I see it. Just three months ago, she was my Dad's secretary, and now, she's going to be his wife. Coincidences like that don't happen to rich men like Dad.

Whatever. I'm going to leave for college in a few months so what do I care? If he wants to spend the rest of his life with a gold digger, that's up to him. So, I just accepted that she was coming to live with us and decided to move on with my life.

"You're already here?" I ask, grumbling as I walk in. I'm usually not rebellious, but Jennifer just rubs me the wrong way. She's not good enough to be my mom.

"Of course, didn't Hugh tell you we're moving in today?" She flutters her eyelashes at me and I want to gag. She slides her arm into mine and I glare at her. "Behave, Mason. Who knows, your dad and I might give you a sibling soon? Would you like that?"

Bile rises in my throat at the thought of Dad having a kid with her. She'd use it to extort money from him all her life.

"Aren't you too old to have babies?' I ask, seeing her expression fall as I step into the living room to find my Dad standing next to a teenage girl who is wearing our school uniform. What the hell, has he already gotten his future stepdaughter admitted to his school? I take another step forward, ready to speak my mind when the girl beside him turns.

"Mason, you're back. Come here, meet your new stepsister." Dad's voice barely registers because I'm staring at my new stepsister, slack-jawed.

Willow stands in front of me, tucking a strand of hair behind her ear as her brown eyes widen in shock. Her shirt is dry and clean, and at the sight of me, her smile rapidly melts away. I don't miss how her chest rises and falls with every breath, nor how sexy she looks standing in my living room.

Holy cow. I'm fucked.

"Willow." I can't believe it. Willow is my new stepsister?

"You know her?" Jennifer asks, letting go of my hand. Her smile tells me she wants to use that fact to get me to warm up to her, but I can't even think.

"We're in the same class," Willow speaks up. "I...I didn't know your dad was...Hugh..." She blinks up at him. I guess she didn't know Dad's surname. My fist clenches.

This can't happen. She can't be my stepsister. Even now, my cock throbs at the memory of her exposed tits. I almost kissed her today, and I wanted to do more. My feelings for her are definitely not brotherly.

"You're Jennifer's daughter?" I ask her, shocked. She meets my eyes, feeling the same surprise that I do. She's not faking it. She definitely didn't know I was Hugh's son. Oh god, how did this happen? I rake my hand through my hair, feeling conflicted already.

"Meet my daughter, Willow," Jennifer croons. "I'm so glad you already know each other. Willow was worried you wouldn't get along."

Willow walks toward me, my Dad's hand on her shoulder. "Jennifer's right. I was worried you'd not welcome your sister, but it's great to know you're classmates."

"Hi." Willow extends her hand to me and when I see her blush, my heart skips a beat. How am I supposed to keep my hands off her when we're going to be living under the same roof? Willow is silent, expecting me to shake her hand. I do, but my heart isn't in it. When my fingers touch hers, all I want to do is pull her in and finish the kiss we started.

"Hey." My voice is low, my body thrumming with awareness. I lick my lips, gazing down at her tits that are smaller than they were at school, but still huge. "Welcome."

"T-thanks. I didn't expect to see you here." There's concern in her dark gaze, even hesitation.

"Me neither," I admit. "I didn't know you were Jennifer's daughter." She's completely the opposite of her mother. Jennifer is pushy and scheming, but Willow is quiet and smart. She's also a lot prettier than her mom. I shouldn't be thinking such thoughts because she's going to be my stepsister soon.

Our eyes lock for a moment and I know she's thinking the same thing I am. It's going to be hard to pretend we aren't attracted to each other.

Jennifer claps, cutting our meeting short. "I'm so glad you two are getting along. Willow's eighteenth birthday is next week," Jennifer moves to Dad and threads her arm through his. His chest puffs up proudly, gazing lovingly at his wife-to-be, and I want to puke. "Your Dad and I were thinking we could have a big celebration. We've got some happy news to tell you both too." My dad rubs my stepmom's arm and fear rises in my throat. Is she pregnant already? Is that what they want to tell me?

"There's no need," Willow interjects. "I've always celebrated my birthday alone. I don't need a big party."

I can tell she's uncomfortable with the attention. I've never seen Willow in a dress, but the thought makes me want to agree with Jennifer. Damn, I'd love to see her in a dress. That's what Dad's gonna buy her. He's always regretted not having a daughter and with Willow here, he'll have the chance to splurge.

"Willow," Jennifer chastises. "We're family now. There's no need to be alone on your birthday."

Dad steps forward, gazing at Willow who looks mildly intimidated by his presence. "Your mom is right. I want to officially welcome you and Jennifer into the family. What better way to let the world know than a big birthday party? Be sure to invite all your friends. Your new stepdad is going to pay."

"Hugh, you're so nice to her. Willow is so lucky to have a stepdad like you." I balk at her obvious attempt at flattery.

They don't know that Willow doesn't have friends. I turn to her, seeing her downcast eyes, and wonder if Jennifer takes time to know her daughter. Or is she too busy trying to land a rich man? Willow hasn't told her about her milky problem. Now I understand why.

"Th-thanks," Willow says to Dad, moving close to me. She's naturally more comfortable around me because we're classmates.

"You don't have to thank me. I'm going to be your Dad soon. I've always wanted a daughter to spoil." Dad's big smile puts her at ease and I'm glad he's nice to her. "Why don't I show you your new room, huh? The staff prepared everything a teenage girl would need."

Jennifer leans up and kisses Dad's cheek and it feels so awkward. Willow and I look away and our eyes end up meeting each other's. Thankfully, we're interrupted by a maid who comes to announce that Willow's room is ready. We all walk to her space. Jennifer and Willow follow the maid while Dad stays behind, putting a hand around my shoulder.

"I hope you'll give her a chance, buddy," he says. "I know you're not fond of Jennifer, but Willow is your classmate. Please be nice to her."

"I will." The words fall out of my mouth before I know it. Dad has no idea that I have a crush on his new stepdaughter.

"Good." Dad pats my back. "Now why don't we go see your sister's new room?"

The news of Jennifer's wedding with my Dad is all over school the next day. There are even pictures of Willow and her Mom moving into the Astor mansion. Everyone knows that she's practically my sister now and her mom is going to be my new stepmother. On the bright side, it dispels any rumors of our being together. After I came to her rescue yesterday, rumors of us being together began to spread. However, with the new wedding announcement, everyone thinks I was just trying to look out for my new stepsister.

I sit in front, Shane twirling his pen in the seat behind me. The class is buzzing, and the teacher isn't here yet. After Willow moved into her room last night, I couldn't sleep. The thing is, her room is right next to mine. Every time I heard her make a sound next door, I wanted to barge in. My mind was filled with fantasies of her milking those fat hucow tits with her hands, white cream running down the sink. I wondered if she was in pain or engorged. There was no way she'd told her mother because Jennifer moved into Dad's room and they spent the night together. She was glowing this morning like they'd had sex all night, and I wanted to throw up my breakfast. The thought of us being step-siblings doesn't sit well with me.

"Willow is your new sister? When I heard you dragged her out of class yesterday, I finally thought you'd gotten the courage to ask her out." My best friend Shane has finally decided to show up to school and he isn't even stoned. I raise my eyebrows and he gives me a knowing smirk. "You kept talking about her after that Chemistry project. I thought you'd developed feelings for the girl."

I clear my throat, unable to deny his insinuation. My head turns up when I smell the scent of milk and vanilla, raising my head to catch Willow walking into the classroom. Our eyes meet for a moment and I attempt to get up. My endeavor is thwarted by my new stepsister who avoids my gaze and hurriedly walks to the last row. She's so smart but she always sits at the back, alone. Willow doesn't have any friends because she's an outsider. Ever since she started going to Astor High, the other students made it clear that they weren't interested in making friends with a charity case. We had two more scholarship students this year, but none of them are in our year. That means she spends all her time alone, reading or listening to music.

I turn back to Mason whose dark eyes survey me carefully. He knows I want her. "Fuck, that's so messed up, Mason. You like your stepsister."

"She isn't my stepsister yet." I know it's a futile argument.

"You didn't deny it." Mason smiles. We're polar opposites but he's my best friend because he's so easygoing. He doesn't judge me and I don't have to put up an act in front of him. Willow takes a seat at the back of her room and when she puts down her books, my eyes go straight to her tits. She hasn't milked. I can see it. I lick my lips as my cock begins to throb. My stepsister gazes up and she knows what I'm thinking. My cock throbs when her face lights up with a flush. I groan, trying to suppress my natural urges. She's forbidden territory and my mind knows it. But my body hasn't gotten the memo yet. "Did she always have such big tits?"

I glare at Shane who shrugs. "Hey, I've got eyes."

A flurry of blonde curls passes me by, replacing Willow's vanilla scent with strawberry.

"Hey, I heard you're Mason's new stepsister." Both our eyes drift to Alanna, the cheerleader who has been following me for weeks. She's interested in me but I've tried to reject her gently. However, she's persistent. She even gave Willow a hard time because she was my Chem lab partner last year. Alanna turns her head to me and smiles.

Then, she turns back to Willow, pushing her ass back to reveal a hint of her pink panties. Alanna's miniskirt barely hides her ass and I swallow and turn back at the sight of her buns. I'm not interested in her. Shane whistles, knowing she's doing that for me. "Why don't we become friends? I've seen you sit alone during lunch and I think it'd be nice to have a new face in our group. We could even hang out at each other's houses." When Willow just blinks, she adds, "You're always reading alone in the library. Doesn't it get boring?"

Her blatant attempt at wiggling her way into my home doesn't go unnoticed. I stand up, trying to defend Willow from her when my stepsister opens her mouth.

"No," Willow says, making me proud. I turn my head to her, watching her stand up. "I like reading alone." Her brown eyes are filled with determination. Alanna twirls a strand of hair around her manicured finger.

"Well, you're never getting an invitation to be my friend so think twice before you say no." She might be trying to be friendly but I know that she is calculative. Just like my new stepmom. I recognize her type from miles away.

Willow is spared from having to answer when the teacher walks in. Alanna moves back to her seat. However, I can't stay still. I walk to the last row and Shane shakes his head knowingly. Sitting in the empty seat next to Willow, I place my hand over hers. She turns, shocked, when my fingers thread into hers. My blood warms at her touch, feeling little currents of delight.

"Mason...." Her eyes move to Shane who turns away. "Shouldn't you be sitting with your friend?"

"You were right to turn her away. She's just trying to use you." My voice is a low whisper as the teacher turns on the PowerPoint. Willow's eyes move away from me. Her left-hand remains in mine as she uses her right one to pick up her pen and take notes.

"I know. She's been nasty to me all this time, and now that I'm going to be an Astor, she suddenly wants to talk to me." I pull her hand in mine and she meets my gaze. Her teeth dig into her bottom lip as she contemplates something. "I...I didn't know my mom was dating your Dad. I've seen Hugh before but I had no idea he was an Astor. I'm sorry."

"What're you sorry for? It's your Mom who should be sorry." Willow raises her eyebrow and I bite my tongue. Of course, she loves her mother. Willow grew up without a dad so her mom must mean a lot to her. Though I'm not fond of Jennifer, I don't want her to think I look down on her family. "I mean, for not telling you."

Her eyes narrow. "You don't like my mom." Her words are a direct hit. She pulls her hand away from me and I regret my words. "You think she's a gold digger."

"No, that's not what I mean—" I pause when Willow cocks her head to the right. It's the most confident I've seen her and damn, I want to see more of these unguarded moments from her. "Yeah. Your Mom and I have never gotten along. Ever since Dad brought her home, I've disliked her. I'm sorry. I know your Mom means the world to you."

I pretend to look up when the teacher begins the class, reading a passage from the textbook, but my thoughts are on Willow. When her soft fingers brush against mine, I look up.

"I don't blame you," she says in a low voice. "I was surprised when Mom said she was dating your Dad. She usually goes for rich men, but it never ends well, so I'm worried. I want this marriage to work out."

I nod, understanding her concern. Willow needs the security Dad can provide, hell, she deserves it. With Dad's money, she could attend the best colleges in the country. I want that for her, but this step-sibling relationship is messing me up. I want to have the freedom to kiss her, to explore her body, and call her mine too.

"I'll try my best to tolerate your Mom for your sake." From the corner of my eye, I see Willow staring at me.

"You don't have to do that for me. You're allowed to hate her. But Mom...she's been betrayed in the past that's why she's like that." Willow turns to me and my heart skips a beat when she looks at me with so much vulnerability. "Promise me you won't use what I say against her?"

"I promise."

I want to know her secrets.

"Mom got pregnant with me when she was in high school. My Dad...he left her when he found out. So, she had me on her own. Raising a kid alone wasn't easy for a teenager. Imagine having a kid at our age." I cough because that's exactly what I've been thinking about—having kids with Willow. Or at least doing all the things that go into making babies. "She was all alone. My grandparents abandoned her after she gave birth. Mom had to get her GED while working two jobs and taking care of a baby." When she gazes at me with those dark brown eyes, I want to say yes to everything she demands. "I hope you understand that's why she's the way she is. She's worked so hard raising me and wants to live a more comfortable life. I know it isn't right to use your father to do it, but I hope you can forgive her."

I nod. Though I understand Jennifer better, I wish she hadn't set her sights on Dad. But for Willow's sake, I'll be nice to her mom. "It must've been hard for you too, growing up without a Dad."

"It's the only kind of life I've known." She shrugs and my heart pulses, wanting to kiss away that sad expression from her face. "Mom and I have always had each other, though she's usually too busy for me." One side of her mouth lifts up in a smile. "I never expected to move into a house as grand as the Astor mansion. I'm happy for Mom, but it all feels so weird. Everything is so…different. I don't think I am prepared to be a part of your world. I couldn't sleep all night."

The room goes dark soon after, and the teacher turns on a chemistry video. Dropping my voice, I turn to my stepsister, whispering in her ear, "Me neither."

Willow inhales sharply, my breath caressing her ear. Our thumbs brush and the ache in my cock increases. I know I'm hardening under my pants and there's no stopping it. I should be good and stop right here. We're going to be siblings soon. I'm torturing both of us by doing this, but I can't stop my body from wanting her.

"What?" Her eyes go wide and for a moment, it feels like there's only the two of us in the entire room. The classroom is dark with just the projector light highlighting dust particles.

"I couldn't sleep last night either. You were in the room next to me and I couldn't stop thinking about how I almost kissed you at school." Willow gazes down and I inadvertently gaze at her inflated chest. God, I want to peel off her shirt and taste her milky tits right now. My hand moves up her waist, my eyes looking around to make sure nobody is watching us. When I caress the underside of her breast, she expels a breathy moan. My nerves spark to life, enjoying our forbidden chemistry. "Did you tell your mom about your milk problem?"

"No..." Her voice is breathy, but she doesn't ask me to stop touching her. I bring my hands higher, gently cupping one breast through her shirt. It's so massive that it spills out of my palm. I lightly squeeze her tit and she bites down on her lower lip hard.

"Do you want me to stop?" I whisper, circling my thumb around where her areola is. I can feel how eager she is to leak milk onto my palms. She shakes her head. So, I continue touching her, wanting nothing between us when I cup those massive milkers and squeeze. When Willow's eyes open, they're dark and hazy. "I dreamed of touching you like this last night. I wanted to burst into your room and finish what we'd started." I know I'm crazy for wanting her like this, but I can't make it stop.

"You...don't regret what happened yesterday?" Her eyes widen when I remove my hand from her breast as the teacher looks our way. I pretend to focus until he takes his eyes off me.

"No." My hand slides under her skirt, venturing up her thigh. When my palm cups her bare skin, she blinks, her lips parting. I want to kiss her right now, but I know I can't with so many people watching. "Why would I?"

"I thought...you weren't interested in me. Weren't you just trying to be nice to me?"

"You have no idea how interested I am in you." I slide my hands up, not stopping until my knuckle brushes her pussy. I feel the cotton fabric of her panties, sliding my middle finger between her legs. I drag it up over her slit, feeling how soaking wet she is. My cock is seconds from leaking, dying to touch that wet little pussy bare. "I dream of this wet pussy at night, wanting to feel it clenching around my fingers when you come." A little whimper escapes Willow's lips as she moves her hips, needing my finger. "God, you're so wet. Do you get like that every time you're ready for a milking?" My voice is raspy, betraying my desire all too clearly. I run one digit up and down those puffy, wet folds, feeling her arousal soak through her panties. I tease her sex, knowing only my hand can give her the relief she wants. It is so dark and forbidden, so incredibly depraved, but I can't stop myself.

When the room goes darker as a black slide plays, I push the fabric at Willow's crotch away. My cock twitches when I touch her bare, slick pussy for the first time. I don't miss the way she gasps, the way she thrusts her chest out to feel me deeper. My bewitching stepsister closes her eyes, her blonde hair fanning her cheek. She's so beautiful when she's all blushing and needy, and knowing I'm the only one who can scratch that itch in her is satisfying. This is a moment that she'll only share with me. I run my finger over her puffy lips, feeling how wet and soft they are. My finger slides up to her clit and when I press on her hard little pearl, she gasps. Her pussy drips juices all over my finger, making me want more. My cock is on fire.

"Mason, we can't do this." Her protests are weak, her eyes closed with pleasure. "We're...going to be siblings."

"We aren't siblings yet," I remind her. "Right now, you're mine, baby." I rub her clit harder and she bites on her cheek to keep herself from screaming. "And I'm going to make you come in class." I've never done something so bad before. I've never fingered a girl in the classroom, a girl who was going to become my stepsister. "If you want me to stop, tell me to stop." Keeping one finger on her clit, I circle her wet hole with my middle finger. When I slip the tip in, she grabs the edge of her chair hard. "God, you're so tight. Are you a virgin, Willow?"

"Mmmm..." Her hips grind on my finger, swallowing me deeper. She's so sexy when she's reacting to me without even knowing it. I love making her lose control like this, love finger fucking her in the classroom. It's a secret only the two of us know. Touching her in the dark reminds me how taboo this is. The threat of being discovered anytime only adds to Willow's arousal.

Her fleshy inner walls grab my finger, the sensation making my cock ready to explode. I sink my finger another inch into her untouched pussy, rubbing on her clit and flicking it to lubricate my way in. Willow is so responsive, so damn sensitive. The way she drips on her fingers, swallowing my digit is the stuff of dreams. My finger is almost all the way in when she begins moving over me.

"More..." Her voice is a needy whimper as I curve my finger inside her and touch her sweet spot. Willow's eyes burst open as a pulse of pleasure sweeps her core."Aaahhh..." Willow closes her thighs, trapping my finger, like she's desperate to come.

"Do you need to come, Willow?" I pull out my finger and thrust back in, feeling her pussy clench around me in desperation. I could've bet she's a virgin because she's so fucking tight. "Do you want to drench your stepbrother's fingers with your honey?"

She bites her lip at my words, the forbiddenness of my words making her hotter. I finger fuck her slowly in the back seat, my eyes on the video. Willow struggles to maintain her composure, her heavy breathing giving her away. We make secrets in the dark, every thrust of my finger inside her a silent promise. The way her tits bounce when she moves her hips rhythmically to my thrusts is hypnotic. I want to swallow her sweet cream straight from those titties when her pussy spasms around my finger. I fuck her harder, needing her to come around me, to put me out of this torture. I want to have every last piece of her. My body aches to touch and explore her in all the forbidden ways before my Dad's marriage is inked and we're tied together by a legal chain we don't want.

"And that concludes today's video." The teacher's voice makes my finger freeze in my stepsisters's cunt. Willow's eyes pop open and she stares at me with undisguised panic. The video screen fades to black. I barely have enough time to pull my finger out of Willow's pussy before the lights come on.

Willow moans with frustration, her pussy still wet and needy as I bury my wet finger in my pocket, rubbing her honey on my handkerchief. Everyone is looking our way and my stepsister pushes her thighs together to hide her aroused state. She's aching from the ruined orgasm, her breasts heaving up and down. Her dark eyes meet mine and I see the need in them. I want to make her come so bad but I can't.

As the teacher asks questions about the video, Willow and I stare at each other. My eyes are drawn to her flushed face, aching to kiss those parted lips. Beads of sweat gather on her temples, her body stimulated and hot. My cock is going crazy at the sight of her. I try to regain a semblance of control and calm my breathing, but when she says, "This can never happen again,", my heart stops.

We both silently turn to the teacher, knowing what happened today is just a preview. I can't push away the awareness of her that sears me like a flame. We might not be touching, but I can feel her pussy juices coating my finger. I scent her arousal like it's perfume. I would take her right here without giving a fuck about how many people are watching. That's how addicted I am to my stepsister.

Willow is my undoing. I need to know what her pussy tastes like. My ears want to hear her scream when she comes for me. When the bell rings, I move away, my dick still semi-hard. As I watch Willow dash away, I know this is just the beginning—the beginning of our taboo, twisted fairytale.

3
WILLOW

I gaze down at the throng of guests who fill the garden of the Astor Manor. Liveried waiters walk around with trays filled with champagne glasses and food, seamlessly blending among the high-profile guest list. Opulent flower displays and bright yellow lights dot the entire garden, making it look like a movie set. I step out of the mansion, feeling like I'm in a Regency novel.

Mom stands behind me, placing a hand on my shoulder. "Today's really important," she tells me. "Make sure you don't let your stepdad down."

I nod, feeling nervous. After spending all afternoon getting ready for my birthday celebration, I feel out of place in this display of grandeur. The entire Astor family is here, complete with Mason's cousins, uncles, and aunts. Mom is dressed in an emerald green gown with matching emeralds that my stepdad gifted her. With her blonde hair in a French twist, she's trying to make an impression. Mom grabs a champagne glass from a waiter passing by and smiles down at me.

"This is where we'll belong," she says. "From today, you and I are part of this world, Willow."

I swallow, gazing ahead at all the dressed-up men and women. Hugh even invited a few of his business associates, taking the opportunity to introduce them to his wife-to-be.

Placing my hand in Mom's I walk down the stairs, noticing that all eyes are on us. My tits feel tight and tender against the bodice of my strapless silver A-line dress clutches me tightly, pushing my tits up to show off my cleavage. With each step I take, my fat tits bounce, drawing attention. I milked myself earlier but my tits are already starting to fill up.

"Keep your chin high." Mom smiles at the guests as my stepdad walks toward us. I'm wearing a pair of crystal chandelier earrings and a diamond necklace that Hugh let me have to welcome me into the family. It feels heavy on my neck, reminding me of the sin I committed last week.

"Darling." Hugh extends his hand to Mom, smiling at her. Behind him, I spot the person I've been avoiding all week. My nipples tighten at the sight of Mason standing next to his Dad, dressed in a black tuxedo that makes him look like a million bucks. His blue eyes glint like sapphires, his blonde hair slicked back. He's even more handsome than usual and just one, hot gaze from him makes me forget that I'm standing in a public gathering. My mind slips to that day in the classroom, remembering how his rough, big palm felt cupping my thigh. When he slipped his hand under my skirt, I couldn't breathe. My pussy dripped like a faucet, desperate for one touch. And when he slipped his finger under my panties and stroked my aching, sensitive flesh, I was in heaven.

"Honey." Mom places her hand in Hugh's, the diamond ring on her finger reminding me of how forbidden our attraction is. Since Mason almost made me come during class, I've been avoiding him. I meant it when I said it couldn't happen again. Though I'm having trouble heeding my own words. Living in the same house and seeing him day and night is wreaking havoc on my brain. Every time he passes by, my body clenches in awareness. When his blue gaze lifts to me, tension thickens the air. My skin prickles with goosebumps, aching for his study hand to soothe my tension away.

"Willow." Mason's Dad extends his other hand to me and I take it without thinking. He walks the rest of the way with Mason trailing behind us, eager to introduce his new family to the whole world. When we reach the center of the gathering, he clears his throat and announces, "Today, I'm going to introduce a very special person to you all." He lets go of my hand and Mom steps forward. "As you all know, I recently got engaged to Jennifer." He raises her hand to his lips and kisses it. Mom smiles smugly, fluttering her eyelashes as the guests murmur. "She's the love I've been waiting to find and I couldn't be happier. We've decided to get married in three months, once our kids graduate from high school." He turns to me and I step forward. "Willow is the daughter I've always wanted. I am so happy to welcome her Willow into the family. She's turning eighteen today and soon, she'll be going away to Harvard with Mason." He turns to Mason and nods. "I'm proud of both of them."

Mason flashes a tight smile and I turn away before our eyes meet. He knows I'm avoiding him, but he hasn't said anything about it yet. My heart thuds as I'm cast into the spotlight.

"Happy birthday, Willow. I'm proud to introduce you to the whole family. I'm sure you'll have more opportunities to get to know them over the upcoming years." A huge seven-tier cake is rolled up in front of me. It's dressed in white icing and I've never seen anything so grand before. "I want you to have the best year ever. Remember your Dad has got your back."

Mom claps and everyone joins in the applause. From the corner of my eye, I watch Mason looking at me. I wish he'd stop staring at me and making it obvious how attracted we are to each other. Before he touched me, I didn't even know he was so passionate. I had no idea it was possible to feel so desired, so hot and wet. However, every night since, I've tried touching myself in a failed attempt to recreate that scene from our classroom. It's his face I see in my dreams, his fingers I imagine when I touch myself.

I smile uneasily, receiving a knife from a waiter. Mom encouragingly smiles at me, gesturing to me to cut the cake. I mindlessly cut the cake and hear everyone sing a birthday song. When that part of the ceremony is done, Hugh takes me around the garden, introducing me to the guests. He has three brothers and two sisters and my head spins from trying to remember all their kids' names. As the eldest son, Hugh has the largest share of the business, which will be passed down to Mason.

As our introductions come to an end, I'm relieved to find a seat among the several round tables with white satin tablecloths and crystalware spotting the garden. Mom and Hugh stand next to me when I sit down. Mason takes his spot next to me, but he doesn't look at me. My eyes gaze ahead, spotting a tall figure in a black suit approaching me. I haven't been introduced to him yet, but he cuts an impressive figure with his tall frame and dark eyes. As he gets closer, I notice his gray hair and hard mouth. He looks like someone important and powerful.

"Astor." His voice emanates tension when he comes to

stand behind my Mom. Instantly, my stepdad's head snaps back and I can feel his spine straighten with tension.

"Anderson, what are you doing here? I don't remember inviting you." There's no mistaking the hostility in Hugh's voice as he faces the man. Next to him, I see Mom go pale. She balls up her fingers into a fist, trying to keep up her smile. The stranger's dark eyes fix on my mom whose hands begin to tremble. The way he looks at her, the way he takes in her body from head to toe, betrays a sense of intimacy.

"I thought I'd pay you a visit. It's your stepdaughter's birthday today." He turns to me, his gaze lingering a little too long before he turns to Mom. "She's a beauty like her mother."

I sense the tension in the air dialing up a notch as Mason's head tilts to me. "That's Dad's business rival. He stole a few properties from him when he was getting started," Mason whispers in my ear, making my body jerk back.

"I got you a birthday present." Anderson hands me a wrapped gift box that's quite small. I open it to find a diamond bracelet in it. It's expensive and I know it.

"You...didn't need to get her that." Mom looks up at him and they exchange a tense look.

"What are you trying to pull, Anderson? We both know you only buy diamonds for your mistresses." Hugh takes a step forward but Anderson doesn't budge.

I turn to Mom who looks more and more uncomfortable with each passing moment. Is Mom Anderson's mistress? Oh my gosh, did she sleep with him while engaged to Mason's Dad?

"It's a gesture of goodwill." Anderson puts it in smoothly. The man has way too much charm. There's something about his maturity and controlled manner that is captivating. "For your future wife and her family."

"Goodwill? You've been stealing my projects for years. You want me to believe you're really congratulating me on my marriage?"

"Don't they say keep your friends close and enemies closer?' Anderson smiles, taking a step back. "I think I'll take my leave now. It looks like I've overstayed my welcome."

"You damn well have." Hugh grinds his teeth. I've never seen him so irritated.

"Happy birthday, Willow." His voice is sincere when he gazes at me and I find myself wondering why. Taking a step back, he bows his head. "Good night."

And then, he leaves.

"Who the hell let him in?" Hugh fumes. "My staff know better than to let the likes of him in."

Mom moves to his side, putting her hand over his. "Calm down, dear. I'll tell the guards to never let him in again."

"He's such a snake," Hugh goes on, grabbing a champagne glass from the table. "Seeing him ruins my day."

"Don't you worry. I'll make sure he never comes back." Mom lets go of his hand and walks in the direction that Anderson went in. With knots in my belly, I look at Mason who turns to me with a questioning gaze. Did he figure out something's going on between Mom and Anderson too?

I sit down, leaving Anderson's gift on the table. It's an expensive piece of jewelry and I have no idea why he'd buy me something like that. Is that his way of asserting dominance over my stepfather? I turn to Mason when his hand closes over mine under the table. My eyes widen, feeling a forbidden thrill race up my spine. He shouldn't be touching me, but nobody can see his hands under the table.

"Relax," he whispers against my cheek. "Dad gets like that every time Anderson is here. He'll calm down in a few moments."

Predictably, Hugh stands up a few moments later. Mom isn't back, but he's had a few too many drinks. He turns to Mason and me and says, "I'll get dinner started."

After he leaves, Mason's hand travels up mine. His fingers grip my fragile wrist, his thumb rubbing my pulse point. My pussy contracts in response, coveting his touch.

"You look beautiful tonight," he says. "That dress was made for you."

"T-thanks." I try looking the other way to avoid his gaze, but with him touching me, I can't. There's no mistaking the desire in his eyes and I feel like a traitor for feeling the same way about him. My body needs him and if he doesn't touch me soon, I think I'll go crazy. His little brushes are making my blood turn to fire. When his gaze dips down to my swelling breasts, I inhale deeply.

"You still haven't told you Mom?" he asks.

I shake my head. "I don't want her to think I'm pregnant. She's very sensitive about that you know…."

"I understand." Mason knows about Mom's past, but he doesn't know I'm a virgin because of my strict upbringing. An odd sense of thrill flicks up my wrist when I realize that Mason has escaped Mom's radar because we're about to become step-siblings soon. That doesn't make me stop wanting him from taking my virginity, though. I've thought about it all week and I can't shake the thought off. I want him to be my first.

"I got you a birthday present. I'll leave it outside your door."

"A present? Today's turning out to be full of surprises."

"Of course, I got you a present. Isn't that what good stepbrothers do?" His voice is teasing and for the first time in a week, I smile.

"That depends on what you got me. Any hints?" I know I'm flirting with him and it feels so good.

"I hope you like it," he says. "It's something I thought you needed."

"Something I need?" I raise an eyebrow, but Mason takes his hand off mine when one of his cousins comes toward him. He dips his head and stands up, leaving me in thought.

I can't wait for the night to end so that I can see what he got me.

"You got me a breast pump?" I hiss into Mason's ear over breakfast, watching the maid walk out of the dining room after she finishes serving us. It still feels so grand to be dining in the long, fourteen-seater dining table with chandeliers hanging overhead. The mansion is grand, making me feel like a princess. All traces of last night's dinner are gone. Mom stored all the gifts I received, saying we could open them together later. However, when I handed her the diamond bracelet Anderson gave me, she sighed, looking unsure what to do with it. She let me hang on to it, but whenever I look at the bracelet, I can't help but feel that it's a piece of the puzzle that is Anderson.

"I thought you wanted one." Mason winks at me and my heart picks up pace. He knows more about me than my Mom does and that makes me feel like we're too close.

"I can't receive a breast pump from my stepbrother."

My voice rises and he smiles, one of those sexy, boyish smiles that lights me up from the inside. It's when he's so light and flirting that I realize why he's the hottest guy in school. His dimples appear and I'm tempted to kiss him there and push my tongue into those dimples.

Last night, I came to my room to find a wrapped gift box lying on my bed. When I opened it, I was surprised to find an electric breast pump signed with Mason's compliments.

Happy birthday. I hope you think of me whenever you use this.

- Mason

My cheeks were flaming all night after reading that note. I quickly buried it before someone could read it. Unfortunately for me, I did think of him when I used the pump last night. My pussy was damp and as the pump whirred, bottles filling up with white cream, I wanted a mouth on my teats instead of a pump.

"Who else are you supposed to receive a breast pump from? Your boyfriend?" The word 'boyfriend' sounds entirely too tempting on his tongue. He glances at my breasts and though I know it's inappropriate, I want to lean in and press my drained, hard nipples against his chest. I want him to hold me like I mean something, which is contradictory considering I'm the one who's been avoiding him all week.

"Never mind. I guess it is convenient."

He nods, turning to his breakfast, but he doesn't eat. Instead, he leans closer. When his lips brush my tongue, I don't want him to stop. "Did you think of me when you used it?"

Oh my god, I love this bad, sexy side of Mason way too much. I want him to whisper dirty things in my ear when we're naked in bed, him buried inside me. I lean a little closer, feeling his lips brush my earlobe, sending sparks down my neck. In a deep, forbidden corner of my heart, I admit to myself that I've missed his touches. I lean closer, not knowing how to reply. Luckily, we're interrupted by the sound of footsteps. Mason backs off, leaving me thrumming with lust.

"Mason, Willow." Mom appears with Mason's Dad, though she doesn't cling to his arm like he usually does. However, she looks upbeat, making me wonder what happened. Last night, she disappeared for a while after Anderson appeared, but by the time the dinner ended, she was back. Her clothes were askew but I didn't ask her where she'd been. I didn't want Mason or his Dad to know. "We've got some news for you both."

Mom smiles at my stepbrother before taking a seat next to Hugh. Hugh grins up at her, but I see hesitation in his gaze. Did he find out about yesterday? Where did Mom go off to?

Mom turns to Mason and gives him an artificially sugary smile. "Your Dad and I are taking a vacation. We thought it'd be good to spend some quality time together before the wedding stress begins. You both aren't graduating for another two months, and we need a break before that." Mom threads her fingers in Hugh's who smiles up at her. Mason's face blanches as I turn my face away. "You're both adults now. I'm sure you can take care of yourself."

Mr. Astor nods. "Mason, be sure to take care of your stepsister."

I almost choke on my omelet. God, the ways in which that can be interpreted. Mason turns to me but his usual bright smile is gone. We both know we're treading a forbidden path. The only reason I never go to his room even though we live next door is because Mom and Hugh are in the house. With them gone, there will be nothing stopping us. My nipples tingle at the thought of Mason touching me and making love to me at night. I seriously need to get a grip on my feelings.

"When do you leave?" He's stopped eating, his eyes ricocheting between my Mom and his Dad.

"Tomorrow," Mom says sweetly. "Hugh and I will take his private jet to the Bahamas straight from work."

"That's...fast..." I didn't mean to say those words but they spill out anyway.

"I know, sweetie. You've never been alone but this will be good practice for your time at Harvard. I'm hoping you two will behave yourselves while we're gone."

I cough. Mom has no idea what she's talking about. So far, she's given me no indication that she suspects I'm attracted to my stepbrother-to-be.

"Have a good trip." Mason leans back on his chair, taking the news better than I thought. He usually grows tense when Mom and his Dad spend time alone. Mom is only thirty-seven and I think he's worried she might have another kid with his Dad. Hugh is 52, and despite the huge age difference between them, they're Truth be told, I think that's why she's taking the vacation. That way, she can make sure he doesn't change his mind.

We eat breakfast in silence and soon, it's time to leave. As I walk out of the door to the car with Mason, I can't help but feel something is about to happen. Something taboo.

4
MASON

I can't focus. I sit in class next to Shane, my eyes drifting to Willow every now and then. The whole school knows our parents are together now, and Jennifer's announcement this morning has me in a mood. A week alone with Willow in my house. How am I going to survive that? The temptation is too much.

Though she's been avoiding me, we have exchanged a few words here and there and I'm beginning to realize that my feelings for her won't go away. I need to touch her so bad. With every passing day, my self-control is getting thinner. I like teasing her, talking to her, and watching those big brown eyes glued to me. I've never felt this way about any girl. I can feel her presence whenever she is near. I feel myself tied to her by an invisible thread.

"Hey, how was your weekend? Sorry, I missed your stepsister's birthday." Shane grins at me, the mention of my relationship with Willow making me flinch. I've been suspicious of Jennifer ever since she disappeared with Anderson that night. I wonder if she's taking this vacation so that she can get pregnant with Dad's child and pull up the wedding. "I heard Anderson showed up and there was a big drama."

Shane loves drama and his eyes twinkle. "Yeah, you know Dad doesn't like him. It was fine, though. He went away after giving Willow a gift."

"A gift?"

"A diamond bracelet."

"Real diamonds? Man, you don't give things like that to people you don't care about." My heart stops. Why would Anderson care about Willow? "I smell something fishy here."

I have to agree with him on that. When I sigh and lay my head down, Shane puts a hand on my shoulder. "Still not over your crush?"

"No." My eyes move sideways and I'm surprised to find Willow looking at me. She averts her gaze when our eyes meet. "She's avoiding me."

"Why? What did you do?" Shane pauses and then whistles. "You told her?"

"I did more than that," I admit, recalling how I fingered her in the classroom. Her moans haunt my dreams.

Shane shakes his head. "Then, you've just gotta face it. Stop hiding and trying to do the right thing. I know you Astors are taught to act honorable and everything, but your Dad isn't married yet. Willow isn't your stepsister right now."

I look up, surprised by Shane's optimism. "Her Mom and my Dad are going on vacation tomorrow for a week. You know what that means. There's no way they won't get married. I don't want to mess up Willow's life just because I couldn't control my forbidden crush."

"Stop torturing yourself, man. Have fun while you can. You'll both be off to college in a few months and all this will be a distant memory."

I blink, the thought of just a three-month affair with Willow unimaginable. She seems like a forever kind of girl, not a temporary affair. But I want whatever time I can get with her.

"It's not that easy."

I throw myself into the class when the teacher appears, willing myself to look away from Willow. But every now and then, I catch her looking at me, and hope balloons in my heart. What if she wants this too? I know she's into me, but is that enough for her to throw caution to the wind?

When it's time for lunch, I walk out of class, my mind heavy with thoughts. That's when I spot Willow in the hallway, standing next to Jake. Jake has her squirming as he places one hand on the wall, blocking her escape. I see the black bag in Willow's hand, knowing she's trying to get away to pump.

"We would be the most popular couple in school...." I hear Jake's voice crystalize as I near them. My first clenches into a ball, a mix of jealousy and anger raging through my veins. Jake is the biggest player in school and the last thing Willow needs is someone like him. "I know you desperately want to be noticed. I'll give you a chance. Become my girlfriend and everyone will be envious of you. All those girls who've been bullying you will disappear."

My shadow touches the base of Jack's shoe, but she doesn't turn. Willow looks scared, her hands trembling. Her gaze lifts to me and her eyes widen.

"Mason." When she calls out my name, Jake turns.

"Mason. What the hell are you going here?"

"Get away from my sister." I react before I can help myself. Getting between them, I grab Willow's hand and pull her to my side.

"No need to get so defensive. Your sister and I were just having a talk. You're in the way."

I turn to Willow who doesn't meet my gaze. "Are you interested in him?" I ask, my tone clipped. She stares at me, blinking. Then, slowly, she shakes her head.

"There's your answer, Jake." I turn to him, my hands still holding Willow's. "Let's go."

I'm distinctly aware of all the students staring at me. Before Willow, I never did reckless things like this but watching her with Jake made anger burn in the pit of my stomach.

Mine, my mind roared.

I didn't want her to look at any other boy that way and I was already halfway to hell.

I drag her away from all the prying gazes, knowing this incident is going to be making the rounds soon. But the thrumming of her heart doesn't stop until we're far away from everyone else. I spot the open janitor's room and drag Willow into it before shutting and locking the door. Darkness descends on us and I blindly grope the wall for a switch. A dull yellow light flicks on illuminating the cramped closet and Willow's blushing face. She's pressed against the door, my body caging her in.

For long moments, we just stare at each other, our hearts beating too fast.

"He asked me out because I'm going to be an Astor," Willow speaks at last. The way her plump lips move is hypnotic and I can't stop myself from touching her. I press my body against hers and she gasps when she feels my erection digging into her skirt. My thumb reaches for her mouth, teasing her lower lip.

"Were you going to say yes?"'

"No." Her eyes are dark and hazy and I feel the desire in them like it's tangible. "I was going to turn him down. You... didn't need to rescue me."

"Rescue you? Is that what you thought I did?" Willow's hold on her pump loosens and it clatters to the floor. I drag in a deep breath. "I didn't rescue you, Willow, I claimed you."

"What?"

"I was jealous. God, I'd never admit it out loud to someone else, but I was jealous because he was talking to you. Because he has the right to touch you, to kiss you, and to know you when I don't."

"Mason...." I don't pull back, pushing my body against hers in a punishing move. When my chest brushes her aching nipples, she moans. I'm aware that she's engorged and needs to be milked, but I can't stop.

My mouth reaches for hers, but I don't kiss her. Slowly, I drag my lips over her cheeks and feel her melt into me.

"Tell me you don't want me, Willow." I rasp against her mouth. "Because I can't lie to myself anymore. I burn for you all the time. Living with you is slowly driving me insane. I thought I could get over this, but I can't. There's no way I can see you as my stepsister, not when I dream of fucking you all the time."

I hear her sharp intake of breath, her eyes melting like chocolate. Her lips quiver and she exhales, leaving my heart in limbo.

"You dream of fucking me?" She blinks, her cheeks reddening.

"Yes," I say. "You're all I've dreamed of since the day I

found you lactating in class and took you away. Before I found out you were my stepsister, I was planning to ask you out. I felt a spark between us, something special I've never felt before." I realize I'm holding her captive with my words. Pulling my face away, I gaze into her mahogany eyes. "I know you don't feel the same way, but I don't think I can stop my feelings."

I feel Willow's hand clamp over mine, pushing her cheek into my palm. "You're wrong," she whispers. "I burn for you too. I've had a crush on you ever since we did that Chemistry project together."

"What?" It's my turn to be surprised.

"I never thought someone like you would be interested in me. I'm a scholarship student and I don't have any friends. I'm not even pretty—"

"Look at me." I squeeze her cheek. "You're the prettiest girl I know. And the smartest and the nicest. I've been obsessed with you since the Chemistry project too. I just didn't know how to bring it up. You always seemed so far away."

"Until now." She gives me a tiny smile.

"Tell me what you want, Willow."

"I want you, Mason." I blink, her honest confession making my cock twitch. "I want you to touch me in all the filthy ways I imagine. Make me yours."

My heart is pounding at light speed. Does she really mean it? "What about our parents?'

"I don't care anymore. They'll be gone next week. You have me all to yourself. Maybe we can use that time to explore this attraction between us."

"You want me to make love to you?" My voice is soft.

She nods. "Do every dirty thing you've imagined doing to me." Her eyes are determined, looking at me like she's made a decision. "Let's use whatever time we've got to get to know each other. I don't want to regret not doing this. Even though I'm scared of the future, I want to give it a shot."

"I want the same thing."

And then, my lips blanket hers. The meeting of our mouths is an explosion that leaves splinters embedded in my heart. It's the total destruction of the good boy I've been, of every forbidden instinct I've denied. I nibble on my stepsister's lips, feeling so right. Her soft body molds against mine, her back pressed to the door. The room smells musty, but I'm too far gone to care. All I can taste are her lips under mine, vanilla and woman drugging my senses. Willow is so receptive, responding to my kisses by circling her arms around me. I push my tongue between her juicy lips, sucking on them before tasting her desire. When our tongues tangle together, she presses her tits to me and I hear her moan into my mouth.

"What's wrong?" I ask, realizing she's in discomfort.

"I...need to milk." She blushes. She reaches for the pump lying on the floor but I stop her.

When she looks at me, puzzled, I say, "I have a better idea."

My fingers reach for her buttons, popping them one by one. I pull her shirt out of her skirt and throw it onto the floor. My cock is hard as a rock at the sight of her beautiful, overflowing mounds encased in a padded pink bra that is soaked all the way. I reach for the back of her bra, whispering in her ear, "I'm going to milk you with my mouth, Willow."

"Yes..." She moans as I undo her claps, letting the bra fall loose. I pull it off her and her massive milkers bounce free. For a moment, all I can do is stare at them, mesmerized. Willow's tits are creamy and huge, with two perfectly round footballs strapped to her chest. Her teats are dark and swollen, her nipple beaded and aroused for me. White streams of titty milk flow down her heavy mounds, making me lick my lips.

I cup her plump breasts in my hands, flicking a thumb over each wet tip. She closes her eyes and cries out in pleasure, feeling my thumbs circle her sensitive teats. "God, you're stunning." I worship her engorged breasts with my hands, gently kneading them to release more milk. "Those tits are straight out of a fantasy. I never knew someone could look so sexy while their titties are filled with milk." Lowering my head, I swipe my tongue over one nipple.

"Mason...." Willow's fingers dig into my hair, holding me close to her aching breasts. I circle her wet, fat nipple, tasting her sweet cream on my tongue. "That feels so good."

"Baby, you taste like honey. So sweet and creamy. It feels so forbidden drinking from your tits."

"It's all for you." She gazes down at me, cracking her eyes open. "Every last drop."

Her words are my undoing. I close my mouth around her fat nipple and swallow it down, gently suckling on it before I latch onto her breast and take my first mouthful of titty cream.

"Aaahhh..." Willow cries out in my arms, a jet of cream hitting the back of my throat. She's so sexy, pressed against the door with those hucow tits hanging out like juicy melons waiting to be devoured. I suck again, drawing in another mouthful, feeling invincible as her sweet titty cream flows down my throat. My other hand gently kneads and massages her aching, full breast rolling her sensitive nipple around my fingers to increase her arousal. "Mason...god...please don't stop."

Pulling her squishy nipple deeper into my mouth, I suck harder, streams of white gold filling my mouth and my belly. This has got to be the best lunch break ever because I want to do this every day. Willow's legs tremble when I pluck on her unused nipple, making arousal strum through her body. My hard cock presses against her covered crotch, fire filling my core. I devour her nipple like a beast, sucking and pulling and tugging until there's no more milk left in her. When I release her wet tip, it makes a plopping sound. I gaze at my stepsister from between her massive tits, pawing her other mound in anticipation.

"You're so delicious, baby. The sexiest woman alive." I lick her other leaking tip that begs for my mouth. However, I know that my girl is soaking wet and I want to hear her come while I drain her creamy mounds. "Take off your skirt, Willow. Show me how wet that pussy gets when your stepbrother milks you."

Willow's shaky fingers reach for her zipper and a second later, the skirt is on the floor. Willow stands before me in nothing but her plain white panties, looking so tempting. "Get rid of those panties. I want to see you naked, baby."

With a shaky breath, Willow complies, lost in the heat of the moment. I watch in slow motion as the last scrap of fabric hiding her skin comes off. Willow's mound is dotted with light blonde hair, her swollen lips peeking from underneath. She looks so gorgeous naked, every inch of her porcelain skin on display. Her tits are humongous compared to her tiny waist but her wide hips and big thighs make me want to fuck her right now. She's so fertile and untouched and my cock aches with the need to be sheathed in her hot little cunt.

"God, you're so beautiful. I want to kiss every inch of your skin and keep you in bed all day."

Willow blushes. "I...thanks." She eases up, no longer so self-conscious.

"Are you a virgin, Willow?" My gaze captures hers.

"Yes," she whispers, gazing up at me. Good, we're both each other's first time. I've been waiting for the perfect girl, and she's finally come around.

"Good girl. I'm glad you saved your first time for me." I kiss her swollen lips and feel her smile under me. "I'm going to make it good for you, okay?" She nods. "Open your legs."

She tits her hips up slightly, opening her legs to bare her pussy to me. The breath is knocked out of my lungs at the first glimpse of her glistening pink pussy. It's so damn wet, creaming for my touch.

"That's the most perfect pussy ever." I slide one finger between her legs, dragging a thick digit up and down her slick folds. Her pussy quivers at my touch, her dampness a sign of her arousal. I love how wet she gets when I touch her. My finger brushes her clit, circling her virgin cunt. A drop of honey leaks out of her cunt and runs down her thigh, making me come undone. She tilts her hips up, desperate to swallow my finger but I click my tongue. When her hands reach for my belt, I stop her. "I'm not going to fuck you today, baby, but I want to finish what we started."

I dip my finger into her wet sex and watch her eyes glaze. She throws her head back, milk bubbling out of her tip. My mouth finds her creamy nipples and attaches to it, sucking hard. She screams when the letdown hits and I push my finger deeper into her, feeling her wet walls crunch around my digit. She feels so fucking good, so fucking tight that I might come in my pants. Milk fills my mouth in a steady drip as I curve my fingers inside her, touching her G-spot.

When she screams, I use my thumb to rub her clit, grinding on her little bud again and again until she's begging me. "Please, Mason….more…"

Her pussy walls flutter all around my finger, creaming as I drain her milky mound. It feels so good so suck on her while I play with her pussy. I push another finger in and initially, she gasps. The fit is tight so I gently nibble and bite on her nipple to loosen her up. I strum her clit and she cries out, letting my second finger in. And then, I begin to fuck her. At first, it's in slow, long strokes, my fingers thrusting in and out of her pussy, but when her contractions get faster, I give her breast one hard suck and begin fucking her in earnest. My fingers penetrate deep inside her sex, grinding against her sweet spot.

"Mason…" She's so close to losing control, her body naked. She's a slave to my fingers and mouth, a puppet controlled by the masterful strokes of my actions. It feels so good to make her come undone, to pleasure her like she's never been pleasured before.

"Grind those hips on my fingers, baby. Let me watch those fat titties bounce."

Willow complies, grinding her hips on my fingers, desperate for more friction. I suck that last drop of her cream with my mouth, spitting her nipple out and licking her swollen teat. "Just like that, baby." Her tits bounce with every thrust, slapping my face and coating me in her cream. I kiss her as I feel her orgasm approach, my fingers driving her insane in a fast, frantic rhythm. She's so close. "Come for me, baby. I want to hear you scream my name when you climax."

I grind into her harder, fucking her helpless pussy with my fingers until she's got no more to give. My lips trail over her sensitive teats, nipping and licking them.

"Mason!" She cries out loud as I feel her fleshy walls spasm around my fingers. Willow comes on my fingers in the janitor's closet, Her nipple grazing my mouth. Wild sparks of pleasure shoot up her core, covering her in an all-consuming feeling of bliss. With her head thrown back, she disintegrates, carried away by waves of pleasure.

I lick and lap at her milky teats, drunk with desire. My cock is going to explode in my pants and I don't even care. I want to feel her coming around my fingers, clenching and milking my digits like she's going to milk my cock. Images of me drilling my cock into her responsive pussy fill my head. I want to come inside her when I take her, filling up that fertile womb with so much cum, she'll be dripping for days.

When she stops coming, I pull my fingers out of her pussy, gently stroking her wetness.

"Mason, that was...amazing." She has eyes only for me. Willow is panting and she looks so beautiful covered in milk, honey leaking down her thigh.

"Baby, you deserve it." My fingers are covered in her honey and I slowly bring them to my lips, licking them off slowly. Willow lets out a sexy groan, entirely naked and wet before me. "You're so hot all naked and drenched in your titty milk." I lean forward and press a kiss onto her lips, letting her taste her juices on my tongue. She winds her hands around me and I hold her naked body close, feeling every inch of her soft, fleshy body. When I squeeze her ass, I feel her pussy flutter against my thigh.

When we stop kissing, I whisper in her ear, "From today, you're mine, Willow. I'm going to use that body whenever I please. I'm going to make all your dirty fantasies come true, baby."

"Yes...." She moans. "Oh god, yes."

5
WILLOW

I watch my mother pack her clothes for the trip, trying to hide the flush covering my cheeks. I can still feel Mason's fingers inside me, his mouth milking me like his life depended on it. We crossed a line today at the janitor's closet and I never want to go back. It's been torture denying him for weeks and now that I've felt his fingers inside me, I want more.

Mom turns to me, her eyebrow raised in concern. "Why are you smiling like that?"

This is the first time she's noticed me all day. After she came back from work, she's been in a mood. Ever since she met Anderson, she's been acting nervous. Did he tell her something about Mason's Dad that made her worried?

"It's nothing. Just school-related stuff."

Mom nods. She doesn't understand my talk about Math and Chemistry and she'd rather not ask about it. "Mom, that night at the party....you disappeared for a long time. What happened?"

Mom turns to me, her eyes wide with shock. She swallows and I know something is up.

"It was nothing." She turns away, fixing her hair. "Did Hugh...notice that I was gone?"

"I think so, though he wasn't too worried. Did something happen with Anderson? Did he...threaten you?"

"No!" Mom's response is sharp. "Nothing happened, Willow. We just talked. He's someone I know from my job, nothing more."

It seems like she's trying to convince herself more than me. "Okay. I'll miss you while you're gone."

Mom turns up to me and smiles. "Me too. Make sure to behave yourself."

She has no idea what Mason and I plan to do once she's gone. But I'll make sure to hide from the staff. I don't want it getting back to her and destroying her chances with Hugh.

"Mom," I swallow with concern. "Do you...love Hugh?"

Her head snaps up, her eyes finding mine. "Willow, why are you asking me that?"

"It's just... I want you to be happy. You don't have to marry him for my sake. I can try for a scholarship to Harvard...I will work something out. If this is about my fees—"

She stands up and for the first time, enfolds me in a hug. "Oh, sweetie, you don't have to worry about that. I'll make sure you can follow your dreams."

Mom isn't the most attentive when it comes to my emotional needs but she's always supported my ambitions. She saved up so that I could attend Astor High and she's never really discouraged me from dreaming big.

"Why did he give me that diamond bracelet? I mean, it must've cost a fortune. He doesn't even know me."

"It was to rile up your stepfather." Mom presses her lips

together. "I will return it to him once I'm back from vacation."

She seems reluctant to talk about Anderson, so I give her a hug instead. She puts her arms around me, lost in thoughts. "I'm sorry I've been busy since we moved in. Are you getting along with your stepbrother? I didn't want to leave you alone with him, not when I know he hates me."

Guilt prickles in my chest at the memory of what we did in the janitor's closet tonight. My nipples are still sore from his sucking, but god, I want to do it again.

"He doesn't hate you. He's just trying to protect his Dad."

"I know," Mom sighs. "Be safe while I'm gone, okay?"

I nod and when we break the hug, I silently slink back to my room.

———

The clock needles are loud as I do my homework with Mason in my room. Awareness prickles through me, knowing we're all alone in my room with our parents having dinner downstairs. After I came back from school and spoke to Mom, I couldn't stop thinking about what Mason and I did in the janitor's closet. We ate dinner together and I completely failed to hide how attracted I was to my stepbrother-to-be. It feels forbidden to think of him in those terms. I could still feel his fingers inside me, making me come, his mouth sucking on my teats as Mom went on about the places they planned to visit during their vacation. After dinner, I told Mom that Mason and I needed to work on our homework together. I'm worried about her, but I'm even more worried about my growing feelings for

Mason. I mean, if it was bad before, it's worse now that I know how good he tastes. I want more. So much more.

"So," Mason's cerulean eyes make my heart skip a beat. I could get lost in them for ages, just staring at his beautiful face. "The English homework." His hand skims the back of my chair and I'm distinctly aware that the door to my room is unlocked. Mom would walk in at any time, but I love the way his hand possessively falls over the back of my chair like he's trying to embrace me. I can't focus on Macbeth with Mason Astor looking at me. My nipples tingle in response to him, remembering how good it felt to have him suck on them. I pumped earlier using the breast pump he got me and it felt so forbidden.

"Huh?" I blink, realizing he's saying something.

"Willow, focus." Mason smiles, his brightness making butterflies flutter in my stomach. He leans closer and whispers, "I know you want me between your legs, but our parents are down the hallway."

I inhale sharply, realizing he's been reading my mind. He places a hand on my exposed thigh, gently rubbing on it. I wrote a miniskirt today because I wanted him to touch me. He has no idea that I'm not wearing any panties underneath and that my wet pussy is staining my skirt.

"You're right." I turn my face to him and Mason brushes his lips against mine. Before I can protest, he seals his mouth over mine. I submit to his kiss with a soft moan, my pussy fluttering when he presses those wet lips onto mine and kisses me hard. His kiss is hot and passionate, and his hand makes me wet as it slides up my thigh and under my skirt. When he brushes my bare pussy, he breaks the kiss.

"God, you're not wearing any panties?" His eyes are dark with desire. "You're trying to kill me. Once our parents leave, I'm going to fuck you, baby."

I love it when he talks dirty. "I can't wait." I lean in and he kisses me harder, his knuckle stroking my wet, bare pussy. His tongue thrusts into my mouth and shuts me up when I cry out. Our tongues tangle together and I drink him in. He's everything I've dreamed of and this messy, teenage love is blossoming into something more. He has no idea I'm in love with him and I wonder how he'll react to it.

"I want to eat that pussy and drink your honey, baby." He rasps when our lips part.

"Mason."

"Yes or no, Willow?"

I gaze at the unlocked door and slump my shoulders in defeat. "God, yes."

Mason sinks to his knees quickly. Before I know it, my skirt is pushed up and his face is between my thighs. He kisses the insides of my thighs, making me leak more juices. "You're my new addiction," he says. "Shane's drugs have nothing over your pussy, baby." He nips and nibbles at the insides of my thighs. "I wish our parents weren't getting married so that I could do this to you whenever I wanted." He buries his face between my legs, inhaling the musky scent of my pussy. I shaved for him and he seems to be enjoying it. Mason licks all over my mound hungrily.

"I...I wish the same." It's the first time I've admitted to my desire. Mason's tongue shoots out and I lose all hold of my sanity when he licks a smooth path from my clit to my asshole, drenching my wet folds in his saliva. It's so darn erotic. "God, you make me want to have everything with you."

"Everything?" His tongue presses against my clit and my hips buck. His hands grab my hips to steady me. "Define everything." His lips close around my clit and a sharp stab of heat travels to my core. My legs are shaking even though I'm seated.

"Marriage, babies, a life together." I can't think of anything but his tongue sucking on my clit like it's a juicy berry. Mason stops sucking on my clit and raises his head. When he looks at me from between my thighs, my cum on his lips, my heart beats faster.

"I didn't know you wanted those things. I thought you'd want to have a high-profile career after graduating from Harvard."

"I want that, but...I also want the other thing....you know, someone to love me. A happy family. I never had a Dad growing up so I want to experience what it feels like to have a fulfilling family life."

Mason smiles. "You're full of surprises."

"What? You thought I wouldn't want to get married?"

"I always thought you'd marry someone stable and successful like a banker or a lawyer."

I shake my head. "I want to be with someone who loves me. That's what matters."

For a moment, Mason is silent, making me wonder if I went too far. "What do you want?" I ask him. I'm guessing it's not marriage and babies.

"Exactly what you do." When I raise my eyebrows, he elaborates. "I want a woman to love, children to spoil, and a warm home I'd want to come back to."

"Really?" I'm surprised.

"Yeah, really. My Mom died when I was young too, and I guess I've always wondered what it feels like to be loved. Most Astor marriages are cold and loveless, but I don't want that. I want the real thing."

"That's...wow." I cough. "I...hope you find someone deserving of you."

"Like you?"

"Mason." Is he serious? I know what we're doing isn't the route to forever. With our parents getting married in a few months, how can we ever be more than secret sex buddies? I might be in love with him, but I'm not delusional.

He blinks for a moment before burying his head between my legs. But he doesn't eat my pussy, instead, he gazes up and says, "I would love to make babies with you, Willow" My blush deepens. "Someday."

Why does my heart feel like it's going to explode?

And then, he promptly buries himself between my legs and makes me forget everything. His tongue devours my pussy, flicking on my sensitive flesh until I'm panting. When he pushes his tongue into my tight cunt, I see stars. I grab the edge of the desk as Mason eats me out, his tongue thrusting into my pussy again and again until I can't take it anymore. He curves his tongue and licks my G-spot, pushing me over the edge.

"You eat pussy like a god," I mutter. "I'm going to come so hard."

He murmurs something inside my pussy, the vibrations driving me wild. When he tongue fucks my dripping hole, I'm done for. I climax with a scream, muffling my voice with my hands. I bite down on my palm to keep the sound from getting out. My juices drench my stepbrother's tongue, the forbidden thrill of coming for him a secret only the two of us will share. I drift away on waves of pleasure, wondering what it'd feel like to eat his cock. He's always the one getting me off, and I want more with him.

I would love to make babies with you.

Why are his words making my pussy spasm even harder? I know I want it, but can I reach out and grab it?

Mason emerges from between my legs, his lips coated with my release. He stands up and I notice that his cock is tenting his trousers. I reach out and touch it, gently palming it through the fabric as Mason watches me.

"Do you want to taste your release?" he asks, his lips glistening and eyes twinkling. How does he read my mind so well? I nod and he kisses me. I suck on his soft lips, tasting how much I want him. He has no idea how deeply I am falling for him. I taste my desire and his, drawing out the kiss as long as I can, feeling him swelling under my touch.

"We should stop." He tears his mouth from mine when we hear Mom's voice in the hallway outside. Hurriedly he moves back to his chair and sits down, both our backs to the door. Using the back of the sleeve, he wipes off my cum and I do the same. Mom knocks on my door a few moments later and opens it.

"Are you still doing homework, sweetie?" Mom asks.

"Yeah." I turn to her, hoping she doesn't see the trails of cum running down my thigh. "We're going to be at it for a little longer."

"I just came to say good night. We'll leave tomorrow, but you call me if you need anything."

"Sure, Mom. Have a nice trip."

Mason glares at my Mom and she quickly backtracks. After the door closes behind us, I let out a heavy sigh.

"That was close." I turn to the books, but Mason stands up. "Where are you going?"

"I think I'm too hard to do homework." I blush. "Let's call it a day."

"Should I—" I gesture to his hard-on and he shakes his head.

"No." He gathers his books and moves to the door.

"Next time, wear panties or we won't be getting any homework done." He reaches for the door handle and I miss him already. "And Willow."

"Yeah?"

"I can't wait to taste your pussy again. You taste so good when you come on my tongue." His blue eyes are sparking with mischief.

I can't even get words to form.

"Good night."

The door opens and closes, leaving me alone with the feel of Mason on my lips and his words haunting my mind. Even when I go to sleep hours later, I can't banish them from my mind.

Making babies with Mason, living with him, getting married to him....what would that even feel like? I gaze at the big house around me, wondering if we'd live here.

I fall asleep minutes later, dreaming of our family.

6

MASON

I'm totally in love with Willow. I stare at Shane who is looking at me with a knowing smile in the library. The library is quiet and empty, but my mind is in a mess. I'm obsessed with my stepsister. I can't stop thinking about her. When she told me she wanted a family, all the floodgates in my mind opened. I couldn't sleep last night, tossing and turning and thinking about breeding my stepsister while our parents were away. I fantasized about running my hand over her pregnant, swollen belly and making love to her while she was carrying my babies. If I thought this was an affair before, I'm sure it's more now. I want her to be my forever, the woman I make babies with and hold at night.

"She's perfect for you, man." Shane is surprisingly lucid when I tell him about Willow's plans for the future. "Does she know you're a sucker for family?"

"I'm not." It's futile to protest. Ever since I ate Willow's pussy last night, I've been in a state. Her pussy was perfect, and getting to feel her fleshy walls squeeze my tongue as she came is something I'll never forget. "Fine, I am. I haven't been able to get the thought of her having my babies out of my head. She's everything I've been looking for, Shane, and I can't believe she's going to be my stepsister."

"You're obsessed with her, Mason. You might as well pop the question and give her the ring." Shane pauses. "You're already in love with her, aren't you?"

I don't even bother denying it. That hit too close to home. I've always been intensely attracted to Willow. She's nothing like her mom or the other girls I know. She's kind, she's soft, and she's real. Most girls of my class are entitled and cold, but Willow is all warmth and soft curves. Whoever gets her love will be one lucky bastard. I want to be that person.

Her Mom and my Dad are on vacation as we speak, but that's not going to stop me from taking her virginity. I've saved myself for her. The thought of breeding her, of coming inside her is driving me insane. I only realized how true those words were when I said them. I want to make babies with Willow. I hope they have her blonde hair and brown eyes. Wouldn't that be great?

Most boys my age are terrified by the thought of becoming a dad and getting married, but that's not me. Despite my demeanor, I've always been someone who's longed for stability. I don't want to sow my wild oats and have a good time while feeling hollow on the inside. No, I want to be with someone I love. And I'm already in love with Willow. Does she feel the same about me?

When I milked her, I thought that I wanted her because we had great chemistry. But talking to her is making me realize that we could be so much more.

A shadow passes the periphery of my vision and I look up to see that Willow is in the library. Her warm eyes meet me, her blonde hair pulled back in a ponytail. Instantly, I stand up, my body drawn to her like a magnet.

"I'm outta here," Shane says, waving to Willow before she leaves. My obsession walks away, her ass swaying in that short skirt. I follow her like a puppy, winding through the bookshelves until she settles on one with novels. I follow her there, coming up behind her as she browses. The library is quite empty and no one is around. I press up against my stepsister, my hard-on digging into her juicy little ass.

"Mason." She turns around and I cage her with my arms.

"Hey, baby. I haven't seen you since morning."

Willow and I quietly ate breakfast with our parents this morning, but when she looked at me, she blushed, remembering how she'd come over my lips last night. I lean forward, brushing my lips on hers. She looks so beautiful when she blushes, her tits pressing against my chest with a sigh. I wind one hand around her waist, pulling her to me and smashing my mouth against hers. My stepsister surrenders with a soft moan, needy for my kisses. Her taste is so intoxicating, so damn addictive. I want her so bad.

I kiss Willow hard and hungry, drinking her in like a starved man. She's my entire world now, the source of my thoughts and my singular obsession. She's turned me from a good boy into a depraved beast who wants to breed her. I taste her tongue against mine, making me lose control. I push my hand under her skirt and squeeze her ass, surprised to find that she's wearing a thong that leaves her ass cheeks exposed.

"Mmmm...baby, you're killing me. I need to feel your cock around my pussy so bad."

Willow opens her eyes, her lips wet with our kiss. "Come to my room tonight," she says.

I blink, realizing how tense she is. She's asking me to take her virginity. "Are you sure, baby? We can take it slow."

"No, I want you," she says. "I've been waiting for Mom to go away so that we can be together." Her fingers brush my cheek, her voice a seductive whisper. "I'll be waiting for you."

"You're a naughty girl." I smile and Willow leans forward, kissing my cheek. Her tongue darts out and slips into my dimple, making my smile wider.

"I've always wanted to do that." She puts her thumb into my other dimple, her eyes bright. "I'm obsessed with your dimples."

"I'm obsessed with every part of you, baby, so we're even." I grind my hard-on against her and she smiles. "I'm constantly hard whenever you're near." Willow kisses my other cheek, marking my dimple with her tongue as my hand gently squeezes one breast. She must've pumped earlier because she's not full yet. "I can't wait for tonight."

I lean in for another kiss but jump away when I hear the sound of someone's footsteps. Our collective gazes travel to the hallway where another student walks past us. We're both blushing, our lips telling our secret. Smiling, I stand next to Willow, looking at the shelves filled with books. My hand reaches for hers, threading into her fingers and holding her while we pretend.

"Hey, can I ask you something?" My heart is thudding, but sneaking around with her is pretty exciting. Being around her just feels so good. "You don't have to answer if you don't want to." Willow raises one blonde eyebrow and I want to kiss it. "Do you know who your father is?"

She pauses like she wasn't expecting that question. The

student walks back up, noticing us, but I don't let go of Willow's hand. When she's gone, Willow turns her face to me. "No. I'm assuming it's someone Mom knew in high school, but if it were important, she would've told me. My father...he didn't want me. Mom didn't tell me why he's not a part of our lives, but I always assumed he wanted nothing to do with us."

Her thick eyelashes frame her downcast eyes, and sorrow fills them. When the student disappears, I let go of Willow's hand and put my arms around her instead, pulling her close in an embrace.

"Mason." Her eyes dart around, worried we'll get discovered.

"You have me now, Willow. I want you so bad that it hurts. I'll always want you, baby." I kiss her forehead and she smiles. "So don't be sad because a jerk like that abandoned you and your mom. He's the one missing out."

"You're good at making people feel better. You know, I used to think you were like sunshine before we moved in together."

"Really? Why didn't you tell me before?"

"I didn't know if you were into me or not. I mean, I was just a scholarship student and you were an Astor. I didn't think someone like you even noticed me."

"I noticed you, all right." I steal a quick kiss, feeling her soft lips under mine. "I noticed you a whole lot to the point it was messing with my head. I still do." I press another kiss to her mouth. "You're everything I've wanted, Willow, everything I've been waiting for. I always thought I'd just go to college, and get married to a cold, rich heiress even though I didn't want to, and I always wondered what it felt like to know someone like you. I'm so glad you're in my life, baby. Now, I know what the real thing feels like."

We sink into another long, deep kiss until Shane clears his throat. Willow and I break apart, but she doesn't stop gazing at me. "I dropped by to tell you that the principal is in the library but I guess you don't care."

Willow raises her eyebrow, worried, but I use my thumb to smooth her worries. "Shane knows. He won't tell anyone." She nods.

"Fine, you lovebirds. I'll go." Shane walks away and I reluctantly let go of Willow.

"I can't wait for tonight," I whisper, holding her hand lingeringly.

"Me neither."

———

Willow's room is empty when I enter at 9 pm. After we came back from school, I was on pins and needles, waiting for when we'd get to be together. I even sourced some condoms and lube, doing homework while the clock needles moved slowly. We had dinner together and Willow looked so fucking sexy in that blue minidress that showed off her tits and legs. I wanted to fuck her right then, but I held on.

Finally, it's time. I knock on Willow's door and when I don't hear a response, I open the door handle and slip in. Willow's bed is empty, the covers pushed aside to reveal the white sheets. I can hear the shower beat, Willow humming a tune in her sweet voice inside the bathroom. I lock the door behind me and place the lube and condoms I got on her nightstand before making my way to her shower. When I open the bathroom door, it's filled with steam, making it impossible to see anything. Willow sings a pop song in her mellow voice, making my cock grow hard.

Steam covers my beautiful stepsister, making my cock twitch. I decide against alerting her, pulling my t-shirt off instead. My sweatpants go next until I'm standing naked in her shower. When I open the shower door, Willow gasps, as if suddenly realizing that she isn't alone. The steam dissipates and I catch sight of my beautiful girl naked, water sluicing all over her smooth skin. Her tits are definitely engorged, plump and ripe and massive and so damn ready to be sucked. Her curves are tantalizing, her soft thighs making me want to sink my fingers into them. Her blonde hair is wet and dark, and her brown doe-eyes are large.

"Mason." Her gaze rakes over my chest, my pecs, sinking down lower to catch sight of my bare cock. My balls are heavy with need, my shaft semi-hard and throbbing for her. Willow stares a little too long, licking her lips. This is the first time she's seen me naked and her open perusal of my body is making me hotter.

"Like what you see, Miss?"

"You're beautiful," she admits. "Though I don't think you're going to fit inside me."

I laugh, pushing into the shower room and she lets me.

"We'll make it work, baby." Warm water falls all over my body, drenching me along with her. Willow steps closer and our breaths mingle in the shower. I reach for the shower gel she's holding in her hand and take it from her. "Come here, let me soap you up."

She doesn't protest as I empty some of the liquid and rub it between my palms. Placing the container aside, I cover her arms in soap. I gather some more and turn off the water, slowly running my palms all over her stomach and back. When I cup her bare ass, she presses closer to me. "I'm going to fuck that ass from the back someday," I whisper against her ear, squeezing her jiggly rump. "It drives me crazy every time I watch you walk away."

She giggles, her hot lips trailing over my neck. Willow is shorter than me, and I love how she fits against my body. She kisses my neck as I slip my soapy fingers between her legs, teasing her wet folds. "Good girl, you're wet for me already." I pull her close, letting her pussy slide over my bare cock. She shivers, the contact making her even more aroused. "You're going to ride my cock, baby, up and down just that." I slide my full length under her tender folds, feeling her slippery pussy sliding over my shaft. My balls get harder and I desperately reach for more soap to avoid coming all over her thigh.

I turn off the water and the cool air makes her nipples harden into fat beads. I stare mesmerized at those plump, engorged tits that are so close to leaking milk. My hands filled with soap, I command, "Turn around, princess."

Willow obeys, her fat ass resting on my shaft as I soap up her stomach, reaching higher for her breasts. I paw at her massive melons, gently kneading and squeezing them. "God, those tits drive me insane. I want to touch you all the time." I run my soapy fingers over her aroused nipples, teasing and circling her swollen teats to make her feel better. I play with them a little more until my girl is gushing cream between her legs.

"Mmmm...that feels so good," she says, her thighs pushed together, choking my dick. She is wet and slippery and so ready for more. She turns her head and I kiss her, sealing our mouths together while I roll her tender nipples around between my fingers. Our skins slide together and it feels so good to be with her. Even mundane things like showering take on an erotic tone when I'm with Willow. My body aches for her, addicted to her femininity. Her soft body moves against mine, making my core flood with heat. My hard cock pokes at her ass and she breaks the kiss with a sharp cry.

"What's what, baby? Does it hurt?" I keep massaging her breasts, realizing drops of milk have begun to form on her rosy teats.

"I'm so tender," she admits. "I haven't pumped since morning." A blush spreads across her cheeks. "I wanted to make our first time extra special"

Damn, I love her dirty mind. I reluctantly let go of her tits, watching them bounce, and turn on the shower. Water covers us and washes away all the soap. Some of hers got onto my body when I was kissing her. The rainfall shower drenches us, but I don't stop kissing her. I push her against the glass wall and devour her mouth with mine, needy for her. Willow turns the shower off with her hand, her ass pressed against the glass, and buries her fingers in my wet hair. When I push her harder, she hooks her legs around my waist, and I grab her hips, carrying her out of the shower room. We don't even bother to dry off because we're hungry for each other. I carry my stepsister to her bed, our lips fused together, our bodies wet and naked. When I drop her on the bed, her tits bounce, spraying milk. She's really full.

I don't waste time, climbing over her and gently cupping her breasts while I look into her eyes.

This is it. This is the moment we come together for the first time. My heartbeats echo in my skull and from the way Willow's swollen lips part, I know she's thinking the same.

"I'm a virgin," she blurts out. "I thought you should know before we…umm…do it."

"I'm a virgin too," I confess.

"What? Really?" She's surprised.

"Yeah, I've been waiting for the right girl to rock my world. I think I found her."

She cups my cheeks with her palms, gazing into my eyes with love.

"I'm so lucky I get to be your first. You're the one I want."

"Me too, baby." I scissor my fingers around one of Willow's tender nipples, getting her milk flowing. "This sexy body belongs to me." She sinks back into the pillows with a whimper, opening her legs wider. I bend over and lick her milky nipple, tasting her sweet cream, before closing my mouth around her areola and sucking hard. Willow cries out when her letdown hits, so much sweet cream flowing into my mouth. I guzzle from her tit like an oversized baby, drinking her nourishing nectar hungrily. My cock grows harder with each gulp, my hands pawing her plump breasts while she holds me against her chest and moans in delight.

"I love it when you milk me, Mason. I love every single thing you do to my body." Willow is hot, her hips rising to grind against my meaty shaft. I gently nibble on her nipple to increase her arousal before sucking even harder. She cries out as I slip one finger between her legs. Cream drips off her pussy, coating my fingers. Damn, she's really ready for this. With another hard suck, I let go of her titty, gazing down at the girl of my dreams.

"Are you on birth control?" I ask.

"No," she admits. "I...didn't have time to get it sorted out."

"That's fine." I reach for the lube and condoms I placed on the nightstand earlier, but Willow puts her hand over mine.

"Can we do it without condoms?" My eyes get so big,

they must be bulging out of my sockets. "I've been thinking about what you said yesterday….you know, about making babies with me." A hot flare of heat stabs my cock. Damn, she's my undoing. "And…I thought we could try it." Her shy eyes meet mine. "If you want to."

"Willow, are you telling me you want to have babies with me right now?"

She blushes. "I want you to breed me, Mason. I want to feel you come inside me and fulfill all my dirty fantasies."

"You could get pregnant, baby." I run my knuckle over my flat stomach and she shivers. "There's nothing I'd like more than to make this belly swell with a baby, but are you sure you're ready for it?"

"I just want to feel you inside me once. Please. I'll get Plan B tomorrow." Her eyes are earnest and I don't have the heart to tell her no. Not when this is exactly what I want.

"Then we'll do it without protection. I've been going crazy thinking about breeding you," I tell her. "The thought of making you a Mommy for real, making your belly swell with my baby and those tits fill with even more milk has got to be the most erotic fantasy ever. I want to feel your pussy clenching around my bare cock when I fuck you for the first time, Willow. I want to be your everything."

"You are my everything," she says. "No one makes me feel the way you do." I reach for the lube but when Willow's eyes twinkle, I cock one side of my lips. "I have a better idea."

Willow sits up and I slide off her a little bit. She leans forward, her heavy udders hanging low. When she grabs them, I groan, pre-cum leaking out of my tip. I'm so ready to fuck my stepsister. Willow squeezes her tits, milking them from root to tip like cow udders. Milk sprays out of her swollen nipples, straight to my shaft, coating me in so much wet, thick cream.

"You're going to be the death of me," I tell her, the feel of that titty milk drenching my cock so fucking unreal. My balls want to explode right now. "How did I never find you before?" She coats my dick in more and more cream until I'm all lubed up for her. When she runs her palm over my shaft, stroking me from root to tip to spread the milk, I groan. "You've gotta stop doing that or I'm going to come all over you right now. Lie back down."

She obeys, sinking onto the pillows. I grab her thighs and open her legs wider, catching a glimpse of her wet little pussy. She shaved her pussy for me today, her bare skin glinting over her engorged folds. I press the head of my milk-dipped cock onto her seam and slide it up and down. When I get to her clit, I play with her, rubbing my head on her hard little bead.

"Mason, I need you." The need in her voice is raw, her hips arching. I slip between those juicy pussy lips, finding her sopping little hole.

"I want to make it good for you, Willow. Tell me if it hurts or if you want me to go slow."

She nods.

I push my tip into her hot sex, every muscle in my body tensing as her tight cunt grabs my dick. "Fucking god, you're so tight." I groan as my cock sinks deeper into her welcoming pussy. She's so small and my swollen girth is stretching her hard. Willow grabs the bedsheets, her knuckles white as she closes her eyes and welcomes the sensation of my cock penetrating her. I lean over her, kissing her face, her lips, her nose, her cheeks, taking it slow and inch by inch. When my cock comes up against her maidenhead, her face contorts with pain. I kiss her lips, squeezing her breasts and playing with her nipples to make it better.

"Baby, stay with me." I push hard, popping her cherry.

She cries into my mouth, tears springing in those beautiful brown eyes. I kiss her cheek. "It's okay, Willow. I'm here." I stop moving inside her, giving her time to adjust as she bleeds all over my dick. My cock is on fire, every thread of self-control on the verge of snapping as I wait. "I know it hurts, baby, but it's going to get better. I promise."

She sinks her nails into my upper arms, holding onto me as she nods, signaling me to go deeper. "Keep going."

I slide deeper into her, my thick root stretching her virgin pussy to the max. It takes us a few tries and a lot of patience, but when we finally get there, it's heaven. Willow cracks her eyes open, giving me a relieved smile as I kiss her, my cock buried all the way inside her cunt. My balls are heavy as stone and aching to unload all that cum into her fertile belly.

"I feel so full," she says. "God, you're big."

"But we fit so well, baby. Your pussy has got me in a chokehold. I need to move." She kisses me and I slowly begin to move inside her.

My initial thrusts are short and fast, but when she begs, "More.", I increase my pace. Willow's body vibrates under mine as I make love to her on her bed, our bodies joined in perfect rhythm. Her pussy acclimatizes to my length as I grind into her. My mouth latches onto her fuller tit and when I take a drag of titty cream, her fleshy walls clench around my dick. "You're so fucking sexy, baby. I love being inside you."

I pull my dick almost all the way out and slam back in. Her fat tits bounce, milk bubbling out of her tips and spraying on my face as I fuck her harder. She takes me in deeper, her pussy stretching. I use my fingers to stimulate her clit as I pound into her, transforming her pain into pleasure. Her body softens under me, giving in until she's raising her hips, meeting me thrust for thrust.

"Mason, oh my god!" She's breathless with pleasure. The way her pussy swallows my cock is so erotic. My mind short-circuits every time I feel her walls massaging my bare dick. Heat balloons in my core, my hands touching all over my girl's body. She's so soft and supple and lush under me, my milky goddess. Milk streams all over her body, running down those heaving, jiggling tits.

"Baby, you're doing so good, God, your pussy is perfect." I nip and suck on her teats, taking alternating drags from each to increase her pleasure. Our sweaty bodies grind against each other, needy and naked.

I fuck her raw, my bare cock grinding against her sweet spot. When my tip hits the opening of her womb, she cries out loud. I drill her deeper, aiming for her G-spot, making her see stars. I see stars too, an inevitable climax building inside me. My spine tingles and my cock is swollen and ready to burst. My balls slap against her ass as my dick squelches in and out of her wet pussy, coating her in her titty milk.

The pressure in my core builds to a fever high with every thrust until it's too much to bear.

"Mason," Willow's voice is a high-pitched cry. "I think I'm coming."

I don't even have time to blink before I'm feeling my lover's pussy spasm around my cock. I finish us both off with one hard, deep thrust that ends in fireworks. My orgasm consumes me, making the heat in my core burst like a volcano. Ecstasy spears through me, pulling me under. Willow cries out my name as she comes around my dick, squeezing and milking me hard. Her tightness drives me wilder, fueling the flames of my climax.

Hot, thick ropes of cum explode from my cock, spraying all over her spasming walls. I'm buried so deep inside her that I shoot straight for her womb. I growl with satisfaction as I breed Willow on her bed, taking her virginity.

"God, it feels so good to be filled with your seed."

"Take it all in, baby. I'm going to fill you with so much cum, you'll be dripping all night."

We cling to each other, soaking in the intimacy. Our bodies are hot and sweaty, fused together in a blissful cloud of pleasure. I can feel her everywhere. My head falls on her breasts, her fingers digging into my back, and my cock pumping her full of seed. She's the perfect vessel for my cum, the woman I want to make babies with, and the one I want to call my wife.

I keep coming and coming inside her until my balls have emptied into her fertile pussy. It takes me a while to find my breath. Willow's cries decrescendo, turning into softer moans and whimpers as we slowly surface from our first intense orgasm together. When I crack my eyes open, Willow is under me, smiling. Her damp blonde hair sticks to the pillow, strands framing her temples. I lean down and kiss her, feeling her pussy flutter around my cock that's still buried inside her.

"That was perfection, baby." I explore the contours of her lips, nibbling and biting on them. "You are perfection."

She gazes up at me, a strange feeling moving inside her dark irises. When I pull my lips off her, she's still staring at me like she's had a realization. My heart thuds, concerned by her silence. "Are you okay? Was it too much?" I hurriedly scramble to pull my dick out of her, but she grabs my hand and pulls me over her.

"I love you." Time stops for me. All I can see is those kiss-swollen lips moving, the woman of my dreams lying naked in bed with me and saying the words I've longed to hear. "I love you, Mason Astor."

My heart explodes into a million joyful balloons, in all colors of the rainbow. The moment is so intense pleasure coupled with intense joy. I kiss Willow hard, crushing her in my embrace. She snakes her arms around my neck, holding me close as we kiss each other like the world is ending. This is everything I've ever wanted.

"I love you too," I say, gasping for air. Though I have no idea how this is ever going to work, I'll find something. I can't lose her now that I've finally found her. "I love you, Willow. I don't want just one week with you. I want a lot more."

"Me too," she admits. "I...I always knew I loved you, but when we came together....it just hit me. It was the most intense feeling ever."

"I know what you mean." I kiss her cheek. "I've been going crazy thinking of you."

I slowly pull out of her, wanting to hold her closer. My cock emerges drenched in her blood and juices, my cum leaking out of her hole. I collapse on the bed next to her, holding her head to my chest.

"I want everything with you." Willow plants little pecks on my chest as I caress her hair. "A home, a family, the 2.5 kids, and a grand wedding. I want to be with you Mason, any way that I can."

I know we haven't known each other that long, but what I feel for her defies reason. It's like my soul knows that it belongs to her. "Me too, baby. I want you to be my forever. I know we're young and we need to go to college first, but I want to do life with you. I want to be by your side through it all."

Her fingers draw circles on my arm. "I'm so glad we found each other."

"Me too."

We cuddle for a little longer before I manage to drag myself out of bed and fish a wet cloth. I clean her up and then, wipe myself off before settling into bed with her. Willow gasps when she glimpses the trail of blood and semen on the white sheets.

Panicked, she sits up. "I need to get rid of this bedsheet before the maids come in tomorrow. Let's burn it."

"Are you kidding me?" I grab her hand that's trying to tug the bedsheet off. "I'm going to save this bedsheet forever." I put my weight on her and pull her down into bed with me. "It's the only memory we've got of our first time together."

"Mason Astor, you're such a romantic." Willow pokes at my chest, but she's smiling.

"You like that about me." I tease.

"Yeah. I like you a whole lot." Willow kisses my lips and we sink into bed together. I hold her close and spend the entire night in her bed, next to my love.

7
WILLOW
THREE DAYS LATER—

I wake up next to Mason in my bed, inhaling his masculine scent. My tits feel a little tender where they rest against his body, already filled with milk. I don't remove my hand from his waist, staring at Mason's sleeping face illuminated by the early sunlight. He's been sleeping in my room ever since we first made love. My pussy is still stuffed with his cum, some of it having dried on my thigh. It feels a little sore, but it's a good kind of sore. The day after Mason took my virginity, I could barely walk. People at school were looking at me funny because of my awkward movements. However, my desire for Mason has only grown since then. It feels so good when he breeds me and when he comes inside me and shows me the fantasy of a happy family life together.

Mason's leg rests over mine, his morning wood pressing into my hip. We've been making love every night and I love these quiet moments we spend together every morning before he goes back to his room. I stir, moving around to ease the ache in my chest. Mason groans, awakened by my movement. I slide up his body, my tits hanging over his mouth as I kiss his forehead. My fingers gently rake through his hair as I bring my aroused, milky nipple to his lips, circling them around his closed mouth.

"Good morning, gorgeous." I kiss his head as he stirs awake, those brilliant blue eyes catching the sunlight. I gaze down at him, my heart swelling at the sight of my lover. When I confessed my love to him, I meant it, so I was really happy when he said he loved me too.

He groans, his lips moving over my distended nipple. "Damn, I must be in heaven because I get to wake up to your juicy tits in my mouth." His eyes open fully and he pushes out his tongue, licking the beads of milk forming on the surface of my teats. The flick of his tongue against my sensitized bud makes my pussy wet. "Come here, baby." He reaches up and grabs my fat breast, pulling my nipple into his mouth and sucking on it. My whole body shivers as the pleasure of my letdown makes my clit hard. God, I love being milked by Mason every morning. His bright blue eyes gaze up at me as he drains one breast, squeezing me from root to tip to empty my milk. I love how addicted he is to my sweet cream and feeding him makes me feel so good.

When he finishes feasting on one breast, he groans. "I'm never going to get tired of sucking on your titties, Willow. I love how soft you are." She pushes me around to straddle him and I feel his cock pushing into my belly. When he slides his hard cock over my slippery folds, I moan.

"Mason, it's five-thirty. You need to get back."

"We've got a few more minutes. Ride me, baby. I want to see those fat tits bouncing while I drink from them."

I've never ridden him before but as I sit over his body, gazing down at the boy who loves me, I feel an odd surge of power. I roll my hips, sliding up and down the length of his shaft, depositing my juices on it.

"God, Willow, you were born to slay men." His cock is hard, aching for release early in the morning. I'm ready and wet too. Sleeping naked with my boyfriend does that to me. Mason sinks his fingers into my lush hips, holding me as he positions his tip over my hole. I push my hips down and swallow his cock, taking his tip inside my tightness. He grunts, loving how tightly we fit together. I thought he was huge the first time, but I guess I love taking my man's big cock.

He thrusts his hips forward, feeling the same heat I feel in my core. His fat dick stretches me, making me feel so good. My other breast begins to leak and Mason grabs my milky mound roughly and pulls me forward.

"Let me suck on those while you ride me, baby," I lean forward, giving him easy access to my milky tits as I take him all the way into my fleshy channel. With him filling me up, I feel complete. Mason latches onto my wet tip and suckles, drawing out thin streams of milk. He licks my nipple, making my pussy clench around his cock until I'm dying for friction. I begin to move as Mason tilts his hips up and thrusts.

My tits bounce like footballs, slapping his face when I ride him harder, feeling his cock scrape my G-spot. My mind goes blank, white-hot heat filling my pussy as I ride him like a wild cowboy, our hips coming together in needy, deep thrusts. I feel him move inside me, feel his cock swell in my channel as I massage him with my slick walls.

"God, baby, your pussy is heaven." He gets go of my nipple for a moment before swallowing it back in and sucking extra hard. I cry out, my climax approaching. Mason's wet dick moves in and out of my pussy as he sucks on my tit with wet sounds. I can feel the tide rising, feel how he marks my insides with his fat dick. His balls are heavy as stones and filled with cum and I want all that baby-making batter inside me.

I can feel it when he loses control, biting on my nipple as my pussy squeezes him into an orgasm. I hear Mason's cries coupled with mine, his fingers sinking into my hips as I make us both come. Hot, thick ropes of cum flood my vessel and I float to heaven. Mason continues rutting into me as his orgasm hits hard. My tits bounce over his face, my pussy spasming and shattering into shards of pleasure.

When I open my eyes moments later, I find Mason smiling, those sexy dimples making my pussy squeeze his dick one last time. I lean down and kiss his cheek, licking his dimples. That makes him smile.

"You're insatiable," He squeezes my ass with his fingers, going still inside me. When I raise my head, he presses a kiss to my lips. "I wish we could stay in bed all day."

It's a Sunday, which means we don't have to go to school. However, he needs to go back to his room.

"Me too," I admit, sharing short, wet kisses with the boy I love. I always need him, always crave his presence. Before I fell for Mason, I never knew love could be so intense. "I want to stay with you for longer."

"Well, I have something planned for you today" His smile is the light that brightens my heart. I love him so much, but as the week passes, my anxiety gets the better of me. I keep wondering what will happen when Mom and Hugh return. What if she's pregnant? I want to be with Mason, but if that happens, we can never be together. I don't want to ruin my Mom's life, but I also want to cling to my happiness. Maybe I should talk to her about this once she's back. "A date."

"A date?" We've never been together outside of our home. Even when we're at school, we sneak around. So, getting to go on a date with Mason feels like a dream.

"Well, of course, you're my girlfriend. I want to take you on dates." He pulls out of me, leaving my pussy leaking his cum. I started taking birth control pills after the first time, but I loved every moment of him breeding me. I wish it could be real.

"I'm your girlfriend?" I ask, raising my eyebrow.

"Baby, I just came inside you. You've been my girlfriend for quite some time now."

I cough. "That means you're my boyfriend."

"I'm all yours, baby. You know that."

I blush, realizing we're both naked in my bed. "All right, what should I wear?"

He runs his thumb over my cheek. "Anything you want. I bet you'd look gorgeous even in a sack."

I blush, falling a little deeper in love with him.

"You brought me to McDonalds?" I look around the empty McDonalds nestled in a strip mall. There's a Target next to it and a discount clothing store, but that's all. I'm dressed in a blue drop top that hugs my massive tits and a black skirt. Mason loved my outfit so much that he kissed me at every red light.

"I can't wait to take that top off you," he said, his lips trailing down my neck to kiss the upper swells of my breasts. I felt so giddy and desired as he threaded his fingers through mine during the drive. It took us almost an hour to get here from the Astor mansion, but I enjoyed the slow, Sunday drive. Honestly, I just like spending time with him.

"I'm sorry, baby. This is the most empty place I could find. I didn't want to run into anyone from school." Mason places his hand on mine, gazing into my eyes. He's wearing a black leather jacket and dark-wash jeans with a cap to hide his face. "I promise I'll find something better next time."

I know what he means. People like visiting those fancy places, especially on a Sunday. If we want to stay hidden, we need to stay out of their radar. We both know we're living on borrowed time.

"No, this is great. I like it." I thread my arm in Mason's, leaning my head on his shoulder. We're pretty much the only two people in the place, except for a silver couple that sits on the other side of the restaurant, sharing brunch. "I love spending time with you, Mason. I don't really care where we go, as long as we're together."

"What did I do to deserve you?" He leans in, kissing my lips. I close my eyes and let him kiss me in public, feeling free and young. When our lips part, our order is ready.

"Let me go get that for you." Mason stands up and goes to collect the tray while I turn to the elderly couple seated a few rows down. The older man picks up a napkin and wipes the ketchup off his wife's face, making my heart melt.

"Here you go." Mason places our food on the table, following my gaze to the elderly couple. When he sits down next to me, he places his hand over mine.

"I wish I could have that," I tell him. "I've always wanted a love like that...a love that only grows with age." The elderly couple smile at each other.

"Yeah," Mason kisses my cheek, and I turn to him. "That'll be us someday, eating breakfast at McDonalds at eighty and still in love." One of his hands curves around my waist, pulling me close.

"Us?" I ask him, my heart thudding. I love Mason, but the future seems so dark. If Mom and his Dad get married, we will never be able to be together.

"Yeah, you and me. I love you, Willow, and I want a life like that with you." His confidence anchors me. How is Mason so sure that we'll end up together when all I feel is anxiety?

"Do you think we can have that?" I ask him. He knows I'm worried about us becoming step-siblings. "We're only eighteen."

"Eighteen is old enough to know who you love. Besides, don't they say love is the most powerful thing in the world? I want to be with you, Willow. You're my endgame." He presses a kiss onto my lips. "So, stop worrying, okay?"

I inhale deeply, butterflies in my stomach. Mason's deep blue eyes suck me in, and I want to drown in them. With him, I know I can have the life I've always dreamed of. He reaches for the fries I ordered and pulls one out, feeding it to me. "Open up, love."

I gaze around nervously. I reach to take the fry from him, but he pulls it away.

"We're on a date, Willow. I want to feed my girlfriend." I blush before opening my mouth and letting him slide a ketchup-slathered fry in. The moment the saltiness hits me, I moan in delight.

"That's good. I'm a sucker for junk food." Mason hands me the milkshake I ordered and I take a sip.

He smiles. "Someday, I'll take you to a fancy place where we don't have to worry about being seen. After all, we've got a lot of time together."

The door opens and a Mom with two kids steps in. The kids excitedly run to the counter, already knowing what they want to order. We watch them as we eat our burgers and drink our milkshakes.

"You know, Mom always looks at rich and famous people and wishes she could be like them, but I've always looked up to ordinary people. I want an ordinary kind of happiness— a job I enjoy, a husband I love, a son whose football games I'd attend, a daughter to go shopping with…just an ordinary, happy family. I wish I could have that life already."

"We're eighteen. If you want to start a family right now, we could put off going to college for a year or two." He squeezes my hip. "You know I'm obsessed with the thought of knocking you up."

"You're insufferable." I smile. "We're just kids. How are we going to support a family?"

"We'll figure something out. Just tell me what you want and I'll make it happen."

"I wish our parents weren't getting married," I say. "I want to be with you without having to hide. I was even thinking we could date in college since we're going together."

"Not a chance," He says. "I'll have my ring on your finger and my last name on your ID before I let you anywhere near those college boys. They need to know who you belong to."

I laugh. "You're cute when you're being possessive."

He pulls me close by the waist and wraps his arms around me. "You're mine, Willow. I'm never going to let you go. Even if everyone else abandons us, I'll always be by your side."

I rest my head against his chest, hugging him back. "I love you, Mason."

8

MASON
ONE MONTH LATER—

I am slowly going insane. I sit across Willow at school, a few weeks away from graduation.

"I can still feel you inside me from last night." My girlfriend says, pretending to scribble something in her notebook. Our fingers joined under the table and my thumb brushes the inside of her wrist, watching her bite her lower lip in response. I want to lean over and kiss her, but we're in class. So, I shield her with my back so that nobody can see us. "You went hard."

"I'm sorry, baby. I just had so much pent-up desire from not coming inside you for over a week." I lean in closer. "Does it hurt? Should I get something from the pharmacy?"

I was in her room last evening after a week-long dry spell thanks to our parents' return. Ever since they came back, we've been trying to find time together, but it's hard. We're always surrounded by people and that means I need to get creative. I milked and fucked her in the janitor's closet twice and the library once, but the janitor suspected something when he found droplets of her milk. We made out in the girls' bathroom once, but I couldn't get enough of her. We've been doing homework together in her room, but that's only.

With the staff and our parents afoot all the time, it's becoming hard to find time together. Willow and I text each other for hours every night, and it's helped me know her a lot better. She surprises me every time, giving me a part of her soul, and I'm a hoarder. I want her to myself all the time. She and I have so much in common. Our visions in life are so aligned. Plus, I'm totally addicted to her body. I can't believe I found someone like her. However, with our graduation approaching, I need to make a decision. If I want to keep Willow, I need to stop Dad from marrying Jennifer.

Dad came back all recharged and tanned from his beach vacation weeks ago, but Jennifer looked brittle, making me wonder what was going on. After they came back, I couldn't sneak into Willow's room for all-night sex any longer. With their bedroom on the same floor as mine, the threat of discovery was too high. So, we took to sharing forbidden kisses and touching when they weren't looking. However, the wedding prep hasn't slowed down. I've taken to finding information about Jennifer to use against her. I'm pretty sure she's up to something because she didn't come home last night. Dad has also been working late at night, making me wonder if things are getting worse between them. On the bright side, it gives me the opportunity to rail my girlfriend without worrying about our parents.

"No, I like it when you're rough." Her words sound steady but her eyes tell a different story. The week without our parents was pure bliss. Willow and I fucked like animals every night and spent our free time going on dates to random, far-off places. But one week with this girl isn't enough. I want forever with her. "I like feeling you inside me the next day."

"Baby, you're going to give me blue balls," I rasp. "Not getting to fuck that perfect pussy every night is terrible for my mental health."

She smiles. We're both needy and desperate and not getting more of her is destroying me on the inside. Still, I'm glad we're together. I got Shane to help me in digging up dirt on Jennifer, but all he's found is her past. He doesn't know who Willow's Dad is or if she's cheating on my Dad as I suspect. When I caught her coming home early this morning, she froze like she'd seen a ghost. Since Dad was already snoring in his room, it was clear she'd been with someone else. Her disheveled state gave her away, but I didn't pause to ask her questions because I didn't want her to know that I'd been with Willow.

"I miss you too," she says in a soft voice. "I'm glad we go to school together."

I nod, focusing on our assignment together before I ask, "How's your Mom doing? Is she excited for the wedding?"

Apparently, that wasn't the best question because Willow looks up, her eyes narrowing. She knows our parents' marriage means we can't be together. "You know, she's been acting strange."

"Really?" I'm all ears. Willow might've accepted her fate, but there's no way I'm letting her slip away. I'm going to do whatever it takes to stop our parents from marrying, even if I have to throw Jennifer under the bus.

"Mom...she's tired these days. She doesn't talk to me. When I ask her about the wedding, she looks weary. She was so keen to go through with it before they went on vacation. Do you think something happened?"

"I don't know," I shrug. "Dad's been his usual self. The wedding preparations are proceeding as usual."

"Yeah." Willow's eyes are downcast. We both know what their marriage means for our future.

I squeeze her hand reassuringly. "Don't worry. I'm working on it."

"What?" she raises her head.

"I'm going to make sure our parents don't get married."

"Mason." Her lips part. "But Mom wants to marry him."

"And I want to marry you," I tell her. "They don't love each other, Willow. Not like I love you. I know it's a bad thing to do, but I can't stand the thought of losing you, baby. Not when I finally found you. I'm not letting anyone get between us. We're going to have that forever, Willow... that house, those babies, that happy family you dreamed of and kissing each other at McDonald's at eighty." Willow's dark eyes gaze at me, a mixture of conflict and need. "I know you want it too. I've spent so much time thinking about it. You're not a teenage fling to me. You're the woman I want to spend the rest of my life with. I won't let you go without a fight."

For a moment, I think Willow will turn away, but she smiles. "Mason Astor, you're the best man in the world." I blink. "I love you too, and you're right, this love is worth fighting for." She leans closer to me. "Let me know if there is something I can do."

I smile. With her at my side, I'm invincible.

One week later—

A week later, I'm standing outside The Royal Palace Hotel, staring at Jennifer's car in the driveway. Jennifer has been acting weirder since she came back from the vacation. She disappears somewhere in the evenings and comes back late at night right before Dad. Since I'm desperate for anything that could get Dad to break up with her, I'm here, fishing for some gold. Jessica steps out of the car nervously, looking both ways and I duck, hiding myself in the rental I got. I didn't want to be traced, so I came alone. Willow has no idea I'm following her mom, and I don't want to alert her before I find something.

I wait for Jennifer to disappear into the hotel before I get out of the car and follow her. I keep my head down, covering my hair with a hoodie. My face is half-covered with a mask. Jennifer is all dressed up in a black dress and pearls, looking like she's here on a date. She looks around and when she spots someone, she stops. I hide behind a plant in the hotel lobby, pulling out my phone to photograph the man in a suit who walks toward her. I raise my hand to get a picture but as soon as the light hits his face, my jaw drops.

It's Anderson.

Anderson is dressed to the nines in a black tuxedo and he extends her hand to her, which she takes. Is Jennifer having an affair with Dad's rival?

They take the elevator upstairs and I wait for the elevator to stop to know they're on the top floor.

"Sir, how may I help you?" A concierge appears behind me and I am momentarily distracted. I quickly hand him my credit card. "I need a room on the top floor of the hotel."

He takes me to the front desk where a friendly woman smiles at me. "I'm sorry, sir, but we don't have any rooms available on the top floor at the moment. Our presidential suite is booked."

Presidential suite? Anderson is really pulling out the stops to impress Jennifer. But why?

"Never mind." I take the card back from her, thinking of another way to get in. "I'll just hang out at the restaurant."

I move to the restaurant, my gut instinct telling me something is going on. So, I take the elevator when the concierge isn't looking and ride to the top floor. When the elevator door pings, I notice that there's an empty cart outside the only suite on the floor. I notice that the suite door is open with rose petals filling the floor. Candles are lit all over, making me wonder if Anderson is a romantic. Nobody would go to such lengths for a secret love affair, would they?

I hear voices and quickly duck behind the pillar just in time to avoid Jennifer who storms out of the room, her hair disheveled. Man, I was late. What happened there in the last few minutes?

"Stop, Jenny." Anderson shoots out behind her, grabbing her hand before she reaches the elevator, and pressing her against the wall. I shove myself into the shadows carefully, pulling my phone out and taking pictures of them in a compromising position. I think this should be enough to convince Dad to break it off with her.

"Jason, please, let me go. I...I can't do this." Tears line Jennifer's calculative eyes. Her voice catches, making me curious about what's going on between them. "I shouldn't be here."

"That's bullshit and you know it. You're here because you want me as much as I want you." Anderson loosens his grip on her hand and she slumps against the wall. She raises her eyes to him as he lowers his head to kiss her. "Don't fight me, Jenny."

Their lips meet, clashing in a passionate kiss. I freeze for a moment, my hand on the record button. I'm pretty sure I didn't imagine the emotion behind that kiss.

Jennifer's body goes limp in Anderson's arms, seeking and responding to his kiss. He slips his hand around her waist, pulling her close and kissing her with need. I want to take my eyes away, but it reminds me of the way I kiss Willow.

Their lips part for a moment and Jennifer says, "We can't do this. You know I'm engaged to Hugh."

"You're not married yet." His hands trail lower, cradling her ass. "Does he know you slept with me after our daughter's birthday party? Does he know how loud you scream when you come around my cock?"

Our daughter?

"He can't know. Jason, please. What happened between us is in the past. I'm his fiancee now."

"Does your body believe your lies, Jenny?" He brings his hand up and squeezes her breast, caressing her hard nipple through her dress with a thumb. "Your nipples are so hard for me. Your body knows that only I can make you feel good. Don't you remember the night we conceived Willow? You came for me so many times. I will never forget how it felt like to have you back then."

"Please...stop..." Jennifer says, but she presses her breasts into his palm, letting him fondle her. I avert my eyes, not wanting to see the steamy scene unfold, but I stay to hear the story.

"I can't stop. I won't. We've been doing this for a few weeks now, and I think we're ready to go to the next level."

"The next level? You abandoned me and Willow. Just because we're having sex again doesn't mean I forgive you." Jason Anderson is Willow's Dad? How? "You left me pregnant at seventeen just because your family refused to accept a poor girl from the wrong side of the tracks. You have no idea what I went through, trying to raise Willow on my own. I was just a teenager and the world is harsh to women like me."

"I'm sorry, baby. I know I was wrong." He kisses her again and I feel awkward, intruding on such a private moment. But I can't escape right now. "I never wanted to let you go, but I was under my parents' control. They said they'd cut me off if I chose you. There hasn't been a day since that I haven't thought of you. I always wondered what became of you and our child. My parents got me married to a rich heiress after college, but I never stopped looking for you. When I found you at Hugh Astor's office, working as his secretary, I was shocked. It was as if fate had given me another chance."

"I never thought I'd see you again," Jennifer admits, her voice breathy. "But that changes nothing. You made your decision, Jason, and I made mine."

"What if I still want you?" His voice is tight.

"It's too late now." Her words lack conviction and I don't have to look to know he's touching her. I hear the wet sounds of another kiss.

"Is it? I'm divorced and you're not married yet. I've tried to forget you but you're the only woman I've ever loved. You know Hugh Astor doesn't love you. He's a cold fish. He'll never make you feel as good as I can. Why deny the passion between us?"

"I need more than passion. Willow needs a Dad, a Dad who can make her dreams come true. And I need a man I can trust."

"I'm her real dad, Jenny. She's my flesh and blood, and you know very well that I have the money to make all her dreams come true. Now that I've found you both, I don't plan to let you go. She should be my daughter and carry my last name. Let me do the right thing. I want to be a man you can trust."

"No. Please. Willow doesn't know you're her Dad."

"I'm going to change that. And it all starts with this."

"Jason...what..."

I hear a thud and instantly swerve back to see Jason on his knee, holding out a ring to Jennifer. My eyes go wide. "Will you marry me, Jennifer? Will you let me love you and make things right? Please, baby, don't run away from me."

I muffle my groan with my hands to avoid being caught. Jason is proposing to Jennifer? This day is full of surprises.

"For me, it's always been you, Jenny. When I saw you at Astor's office, I was struck by the cupid's arrow again, just like all those years ago. Let me give you the life you deserve. Please, say yes, my love."

I can't believe my luck. I've been going crazy all month, scared about losing Willow. Anderson might be the answer to all my problems. If he's Willow's biological Dad, that changes everything. She doesn't have to be my stepsister to go to college.

"Jason...I can't....you know this isn't right. I gave my word to Hugh."

"Baby, love isn't logical. Are you sure you'll be happy if you say no to me now? Will you never regret it?"

Jennifer bites her lip, caught in confusion. Willow told me her Mom got pregnant in high school and that's why she's so fussy about the men Willow is around. However, I had no idea that she'd been knocked up by my Dad's business rival. He's from an old money family, and he might be the only man she has any feelings for. The calculated gleam in her eyes begins to thaw when he's near.

"Pease, don't make me choose. You know I can't break Hugh's heart."

"I'll throw him a deal to sweeten the pot. Just be mine, Jenny. Life is full of hard decisions. You and I have both made them and that's why I know how important it is to choose the right person." Jennifer closes her eyes, tortured. "Say you don't love me, Jenny and I'll go away. Say you're in love with Hugh Astor instead."

She exhales heavily. "You know I can't say that."

"Then, marry me. Let me repent for my sins and spend the rest of my life making you happy."

Damn, I never realized he was such a romantic. Jennifer hesitates for a long moment, her eyes turning desperate and watery. But a few seconds later, she finally says the word Anderson and I have been dying to hear.

"You promise you'll never leave me?" Jennifer asks.

"Never. You're mine forever. I won't let you go until the day I die."

Jennifer sighs. "Fine. Yes. I'll marry you." Anderson's face lights up with a smile. I don't think I've ever seen him look so happy. "Though I have no idea how I'm going to explain this to Willow and the Astors."

"I'll take care of that." Anderson stands up and slips the ring onto her finger. He pulls her in and kisses her. "All that matters is that you're mine now."

I wait for their kiss to turn steamy. Soon, they move back to the hotel room and the door closes shut. Peeling myself off the pillar, I hurriedly take the elevator downstairs. My heart hammers in my chest, excited to know that Willow is no longer going to be my stepsister. I want to go to her, tell her the truth, and make love to her all night. But I guess I'm going to have to wait until Jennifer delivers the news to her.

I walk out of the hotel, my heart a ton lighter. Looks like I've got my own proposal to plan.

9
WILLOW

It's the week of graduation and I make my way back home with Mason in his Dad's car. So far, it doesn't seem like we've made any progress on getting Mom and Hugh to break up, and with each passing day, my anxiety increases. I'm so in love with Mason. I want to be his for the rest of my life, but how?

"Are you okay?" he asks, squeezing my hand. He presses the button that turns up the screen that blocks the driver's view of us.

"Yeah, I'm just nervous about...us."

"Trust me, I'm working on it, baby." Mason slides closer to me, putting his hand around my shoulder. For a moment, I think he's going to say something, but he doesn't. Instead, he kisses me. The moment his lips touch mine, all my anxiety disappears. We kiss deep and hard, my body needing him, as always. I've gotten used to his presence. He's my anchor in the chaos.

With a wet kiss, he lets me go, sliding his lips down my jaw and kissing my neck. "You don't have to worry, Willow. I think everything is going to turn out just fine."

"You think so?" my mind is in a blur. We've been having sex and sneaking around quite a lot. Mom and Hugh have both been coming home late, and that means I get to spend more time with Mason. I never want this to end.

"Yeah, baby." He sucks on the sweet spot at the base of my neck and my pussy pulses in response. My arms loop around his back and I feel his solid weight as he licks and pleasures my sensitive spot.

The car slows down and reluctantly, Mason pulls his mouth away. "I've got something to tell you. Meet me in my room later, okay?"

I nod as he wipes his spit from my neck to hide his tracks. Hopefully, we won't have to hide much longer. I know we're going to college together but I want the whole world to know that I belong to him.

The driver gets off and opens the door for us and we both walk out, hand-in-hand. However, when I see Mom's car in the driveway, I drop Mason's hand. He gives me a confused look and we both walk in to find Mom sitting in the living room.

"Willow, you're back." Mom's eyes bulge, a little too eager. I wonder why she's back from work so early. Did she forget something at home? Before I can ask, a tall figure next to her stands.

"Good afternoon." Anderson is standing there, dressed in a navy suit and red tie. He looks as charismatic as ever, his tall form making me feel weird. His dark brown eyes shift from me to Mason, who doesn't look as tense as he did the first time. "We were waiting for you to get back from school."

"Willow, I want to talk to you." She turns to Anderson, who shakes his head, turning to Mason.

"In private, please."

"I'll go get changed." Mason steps back, not viewing Mom with hostility for the first time. It's strange to have Anderson in the house, especially because Hugh hates him. Once Mason is gone, I turn to my mother.

"Where's Hugh?" I ask, looking around.

"He's at work. He'll be coming home in a few hours. We wanted to talk to you before he got here."

"We?" I drop my bag, remaining standing. Mom and Anderson don't sit either.

A wedding ring glints on Mom's finger. I know the diamond Hugh gave her was huge, but she isn't wearing that one. Instead, she has an emerald ring framed with diamonds on her ring finger. My eyes widen, my mind conjuring up worst-case scenarios.

"That doesn't look like the ring Hugh gave you." My tone is sharp and accusatory.

"Willow, sit down, honey." Mom tries to touch me but I back off, dropping my ass on the couch. Mom and Anderson sit down together, and he gently lays his palm on top of hers, squeezing. My heart begins to hammer in my chest. God, this can't be true. Has mom been cheating? Though I'm keen to break up Mom and Mason's Dad, a cheating scandal is the last thing I need. It would break Mason's heart.

"There's something Jason and I want to tell you." Jason? Oh god, she's calling Anderson by his first name.

"We're getting married." He announces, smiling at me happily. I've never seen Anderson look so happy. What is going on here?

"But...I thought you were marrying Hugh. Isn't that why we're living here?"

"About that." Mom swallows. "I'm going to break off my engagement with Mason's Dad." She looks at Anderson and I see the one thing I've never seen in my mother's eyes—love. My heart stops for a moment, wondering if this is even real. I've been praying for a miracle, praying for a way to be with Mason as his girlfriend and it looks like the heavens have answered my prayers. If Mom and Anderson get married, Mason and I can be together, and that makes me perk up.

"You love him." My tone is serious and Mom meets my eyes.

"More than I've ever loved anyone in my life," Mom says. "I thought we'd lost our chance together, but when he reappeared in my life, something in my heart shifted. I wanted to deny what I was feeling but I couldn't. I'm sorry I had to keep this from you, Willow. When Jason came to the party, I was shaken. You can hate me for going behind Hugh's back, but I don't regret it."

"I don't blame you, Mom. I'm happy for you, really." Maybe Mason was right. Mom isn't really in love with Hugh and marrying Anderson definitely seems like the better choice. I've never seen her so happy before. She's glowing like a bride.

"Thank you, dear. I was so worried you'd hate me for breaking it off with Mason's Dad. You and your stepbrother get along so well." I cough, wondering if she knows what kind of relationship Mason and I share.

"Hey, I'm partially to blame too," Anderson says. "I pursued your Mom relentlessly until she gave in. I know Hugh isn't going to be happy about this, but I'm so glad she said yes."

"Are you planning to tell Hugh?" I ask them.

"Once he arrives," Anderson says. "We've been rivals for ages so I don't expect him to take this well. He'll think I'm trying to steal his bride." He looks at my Mom and his eyes are filled with love. I never knew you could fall in love with someone so fast, but hey, Mason and I are a case in point. "I'm willing to lose a few of my projects to him if it helps. After all, it is because of him that I found Jennifer again."

"You guys knew each other?" I ask, wondering if they have any history.

"Your Mom and I went to high school together. She was the love of my life."

That gives me pause. The guy who got Mom pregnant and broke her heart also went to high school with her. Mom realizes what I'm thinking and leans forward.

"There's something else we want to tell you too," Mom begins in a soft voice. She threads her fingers through Anderson's and he turns his dark eyes to me. "I never told you who your father was. I think it's time to reveal that secret."

My jaw drops.

And suddenly, it all becomes clear.

The diamond bracelet, Anderson's dark eyes that look so much like mine, his deep connection with my Mom. He is my Dad.

"Jason and I...we used to date in high school." She gets the words out laboriously. "We..." When she pauses, Anderson takes over.

"We were in love," he admits. "Your Mom was the love of my life. Still is. She was so different from me. We were like chalk and cheese, but I couldn't stop myself from falling for her. I'd never met anyone like her and...even though our backgrounds were different, we fell in love hard and fast."

Tears prick the back of my eyes.

"You're my father." The words fall out of my mouth before I can stop myself. There's no calming the chaos in my heart. For so many years, I've wondered who my Dad was. But Anderson? I never even dreamed it could be him. Now that I look at him, he has my dark eyes and that straight nose. God, how did I miss it?

He smiles at me. "Yes."

Just like that, my whole world comes to a halt.

"I'm sorry, Willow. I never wanted to abandon you or your Mom. But my parents were against the match. They said Jenny didn't belong in our world. I wanted to fight for our love but they threatened to cut me out if I chose her and...." He sighs. "I guess I was too weak. I didn't want to lose everything I had. Back then, becoming someone successful was more important to me than protecting our love. I was so wrong. When I saw Jenny again, I knew how stupid I'd been. If I could go back to that time, I'd choose her."

"You're my father," I repeat the words in disbelief. "But...how...why...why did you never come to see me?"

"We lost touch after high school." Mom leans forward. "I moved away because I wanted to cut off all ties with Jason. I was angry because he'd chosen his family over me and I never quite got over the heartbreak. For years, I resented everyone because I'd been abandoned by the man I gave my heart to." Jason squeezes her hand, pulling it up to his lips for a kiss.

"I'm so sorry. If I'd been stronger, the both of you could've avoided so much pain. It's all my fault, but I promise I'll make it okay. Willow, you're my heir. Once your mom and I talk to Hugh, you'll move into my house and have the life you were always meant to live. Your mom said you're going to Harvard, and I want you to have the best experience ever."

Woah, this is moving too fast. "I'm sorry I couldn't be

there for you while you were growing up. After my divorce, I tried looking for your Mom, but I couldn't find her. So, when I saw Jenny again at Astor's office, I thought it was a miracle. You're the only family I've ever wanted, and I promise that I'll do everything to make sure you never miss having a Dad. You don't have to forgive me, but I love you, Willow, even though I've only known you for a short time. My daughter...god, I am so lucky because I get to have both of you."

Anderson and Mom stand up and I feel emotionally raw as my mother opens her arms. She's the happiest I've seen her, and I can't believe she rekindled things with my Dad. He left a huge hole in her heart when he left, but with him back in her life, everything seems to be settled. Mom and Anderson hold their hands open for me and I hug them. A tear falls from my eye when I realize that I'm hugging my Dad for the first time. All this time, I thought he didn't want me, but he was looking for us.

"I love you, Willow," he says. "I'm going to make your Mom really happy. I'll give you everything you want, you just have to ask. I promise I'll try to be a good Dad to you."

I don't say anything as we remain locked in a hug. When we break apart, Anderson says, "Thanks for giving me a chance, Willow."

I turn to my Mom and know that this is the right thing to do. Seeing her happy is so worth it. Besides, this means I can be with the love of my life too.

Mason.

Oh my gosh. I can't wait to tell him about this.

When there's a sound at the entrance, I step back.

"Looks like Hugh is here," Mom says, turning to me. "Willow, why don't you go upstairs and wait for us? We might need to pack our bags after this conversation."

I nod, rushing upstairs with excitement filling my heart. All I can think of is the fact that Mason and I can finally be together.

When I open the door to Mason's room, my jaw drops. I've been downstairs for less than an hour and in that time, Mason has managed to turn his room into a romantic date spot. Candles surround us, a bouquet of flowers sitting in the vase on his table. His bed is covered in creaseless, neat white sheets, and Mason stands at the edge, dressed up with a bouquet of roses in his hand.

"Mason, what's going on?" I meet his eyes that are filled with love and my heart gives a lurch. He knows everything. "You knew."

My boyfriend walks toward me, giving me the bouquet. I accept it from him wordlessly, my heart thudding as the scent of red roses fills the air. "About your Mom and Anderson? Yeah. I saw them leaving the hotel together and figured it out."

"Did you also know that...." Mason's eyes darken. "He's my Dad."

"Yeah. At first, I wanted to strangle him for abandoning you, but then again, it's thanks to his timely appearance that we don't have to become step-siblings. But if you want me to make him pay—"

"No, I...I thought the same thing." I stand in my uniform, looking around the room. "So, what's this about?"

I hear the sound of raised voices downstairs. Hugh must be getting mad at Mom, but my attention is entirely focused on Mason.

"Now that our parents won't be getting married, I

thought it was time to move our relationship to the next stage." I blink as Mason goes down on one knee, fishing out a velvet box from his shirt pocket. He flips the box open and a diamond ring shines up at me.

"Mason...."

"Willow, will you marry me? Will you be my wife, my forever companion, and the mother of my children?" Tears of joy fill my eyes instantly, making Mason's form blur before me. "I want us to attend college as a couple, and I promise baby, I'll always make you happy, no matter what it takes."

My lips tremble, unable to believe that this is really happening. I was so scared about losing Mason, but this changes everything.

"Yes!" I cry out. "I will marry you, Mason Astor."

Mason's bright smile makes my entire day. He slips the ring onto my finger and then stands up to fold me in a hug. We kiss hard, oblivious to the loud quarrel downstairs. I don't even care about it anymore. All that matters is that I'm here now, in the arms of the boy I love.

"I love you, Willow," Mason says when our lips part. "I want to spend the rest of my life with you, baby."

"Me too," I say. "I've never loved anyone as much as you. I'm just so glad we can finally be together."

We kiss again, and I ask, "Does your Dad know?"

"Not yet," Mason says. "I was thinking we could wait until graduation to tell them. It's going to take that long for them to calm down. Dad's gonna need me to console him once your Mom breaks the news of her engagement to Anderson."

"I'm really sorry about that," I say. "Though I'm glad Mom found her love, I wish she didn't have to hurt your Dad. He's always been nice to me."

"It's okay. He'll get over it." Mason kisses my nose. "I'm going to miss not having you around in the house."

"Maybe I can move in once we get married."

He smiles. "I'd love that."

We kiss again and again, forgetting time and space. When my swollen lips emerge, I stare into the turquoise eyes of the love of my life. I'm glad it all turned out well in the end.

10

MASON
SIX YEARS LATER—

I caress my wife's seven-month-old baby bump in our bed, watching the sun fade outside the window of the Astor mansion. After Willow and I graduated from Harvard, we moved back in to help Dad with his business. Now that I have an official position in the company, I get to do more meaningful work. The fact that Willow also works with me is just the icing on the cake.

"I can't believe we're here again," Willow says, leaning back on my bare chest and letting me kiss her long- blonde hair. My wife's done with work and we're all ready for the night. Her black tank top hugs her massive mommy milkers that spill out of the hem, her wet, hard nipples outlined against the fabric. The fabric molds around her massive stomach, leaving no doubt about her condition.

"Me neither," I kiss my wife's temple as her hands explore my chest. I love sitting in bed with her and touching her pregnant body before we make love all night. My bulge presses on her back, making her rub her legs together in anticipation. Her shorts sink into the crack of her ass, framing her pussy lips. Willow has filled out and become even more beautiful since she got pregnant. "This is where everything started. How does it feel to be here, Mrs. Astor?"

"It's the best feeling in the world." Her brown eyes are filled with warmth and I want to lose myself in them. Willow and I went to college together, even staying in the same apartment during our four years there. I'm pretty sure we've had sex on every surface in that apartment along with stealing kisses in between classes. I can't keep my hands off my hot, sexy wife.

We've been married for six years. After I proposed to her, I waited until we graduated to tell Dad that I was in love with Willow and going to marry her. He was shocked initially but after Jennifer and he broke up, we had some time to bond and so, he finally accepted.

"I liked her, even though her Mom and I didn't work out. Though I'm not keen to be in-laws with Anderson."

Anderson had given up one of his lucrative properties to pacify Dad. Jennifer and Willow moved into Anderson's house the day after I proposed to Willow. They got married a month later, just after we graduated. Jennifer gave birth to Willow's brother four years ago, making him Anderson's official heir. Willow has been bonding with her Dad ever since our marriage and they've grown closer over time. He wanted her to come to work for him, but she chose to work at Dad's company instead so that we could stay close. Dad's relationship with Anderson has improved too and they're not the bitter rivals they used to be. He loves Willow, and perhaps that's why he tolerates her Dad.

Willow turns her head and says in a soft voice, "I'm so excited to meet our baby." She places her soft hand on mine. I pull the hem of her top up, laying my hand on her bare stomach.

"Me too," I tell her. "I've wanted to make babies with you ever since I first saw you. I guess this is the beginning of all our dreams coming true."

Though it's been six years since I married Willow, I still crave her like we're newlyweds. My wife is the sexiest woman alive and I only love her body more and more with each passing year. We decided to wait until we graduated to have kids. It was a torturous wait, especially because I love breeding my wife and ached to see her swollen with my child. The day we graduated, I took her to our bedroom and bred her all night, hoping she'd get pregnant. It took us a while to get there, but I'm so happy that we're finally starting our own family.

"You're everything I've ever wanted, Willow. I can't believe you're mine." My hand stills on her belly as she turns her face, meeting my lips in a soft, loving kiss. Lust spikes in my blood the moment our mouths fuse together and I hungrily kiss her lips, pushing her back onto the bed. Willow reaches for my shorts and peels them off to reveal my thick, engorged cock that's always hard for my sexy, milky wife. I pull off her shorts, running one thick finger over her plump, wet folds. She raises her hand and I pull her top off, letting her massive milkers bounce free. She's already leaking, her swollen, fat tips lined with cream.

"Baby, you're so sexy when you're lactating with that belly filled with a baby." My lips drift over her plump, ripe tits, licking the cream off her tips. My mouth ventures lower, kissing the curve of her breasts and then, that beautiful, swollen belly. My hot mouth travels all over her swollen stomach, kissing every inch of her skin as I encase her pregnant stomach in my big palms. "God, you're so sexy with that big belly, I want to keep you knocked up forever. I love breeding you, Mrs. Astor."

"And I love being bred by you, Mr. Astor." Her dark eyes gaze down at me, filled with undisguised lust. Her titties are leaking and hungry for my mouth. I stop worshipping her stomach, knowing my girl needs me.

"Ready to be milked by your husband, Willow?"

"Always."

I close my mouth around one stiff peak and swallow it down, suckling to get her milk flowing. Milk gushes into my mouth like a geyser and I gulp it all down, loving her familiar taste. Soon, our son will be nursing from her soft, plush tits, but until then, she's all mine.

"God, Mason, more." Her legs wrap around my waist and she slides her fingers into my hair, loving how I milk her in bed. I've kept her filled with milk all these years, feasting on her twice a day to keep her body producing that delicious titty cream. She's my milky addiction.

"You're all mine, baby. You're all mine, baby. My wife, my love, the mother to my children, and my milky addiction. I'm going to keep you in bed all night and fuck that body like it deserves."

"Yes…" She's breathless.

I cup and squeeze her other breast. Milk streams down her big belly, covering my wife in her forbidden cream. When my thumb slides over her beaded nipples, she moans hard, arching her back and pushing that delectable teat deeper between my lips. I lick and gently bite down on her tip, greedily consuming her titty cream. She's gotten so sensitive since she became pregnant and I love giving my wife the relief she needs.

My fingers slip between her legs, gently teasing her creamy folds and I fill my mouth with her cream. When I'm done with one breast, I latch onto the other. Her screams fill the room as her letdown hits. My fingers roll her clit around, playing with her little bead while I milk my wife. Every stream of milk in my mouth is proof of her devotion to me, of her fertile body getting ready to nourish the baby we created with our love.

"Mason...please..." My wife spreads her legs, beckoning me deep into her fertile body with needy moans. "I need you inside me."

I pop her nipple out, giving it one last lick before I command, "On your hands and feet, honey. Show me how needy that pussy is."

Willow complies. The moment she gets on all fours, that sexy ass thrusting up, and those massive titties hanging low like overripe melons, I can't hold my lust in any longer. I climb behind my wife and sink my fingers into her generous hips, lining up my cock head with her sopping hole.

"I love you, baby. I love you so much." My words are raspy as I push into her fleshy channel, swallowed up by her hot, pulsing cunt. Darts of pleasure shoot from my cock to my core, making my balls feel heavy with the need to come. "You're so perfect, so fucking tight, and you're all mine, Willow." My cock delves deep into her, and I taste a slice of heaven. The way her walls ripple around me is so damn erotic. "Now, let me show you how good I fuck the pussy I own."

I begin moving inside her with deep, hard thrusts, just the way she loves. Willow is always wet and eager, ready to take me and I am so lucky to be with a woman who mirrors my passionate desire.

"God...yess...Mason....more....." Willow cries out as I pound into her ruthlessly. Her tits jiggle, spraying milk on the sheets as her big belly bounces with every hard, deep thrust. I scrape her G-spot with the tip of my cock, skyrocketing her pleasure. I know all her sweet spots, all the ways to get her off. And I love the familiarity we share. It makes our lovemaking even better. My cock drills into her fertile cunt, pleasure sparking everywhere until we're both on the verge of an orgasm. "I'm coming, baby...."

"Yes, come around me, wife," I growl as I fuck her so deep, I touch her fertile womb. "Show me what a good girl you are."

Willow's pussy spasms around my cock and her screams fill the air. She calls out my name as she is swallowed up by the first wave of her orgasm. I can feel her tight pussy squeezing me in a death grip, milking me for my seed.

"I'm coming too, baby." My voice is a torn growl as I surrender to an obliterating climax inside my wife. My cock swells inside her and bursts into ropes of hot cum.

"Mason...yes...come inside me. Fill me up with your seed." It's so sexy the way she begs to be bred, even though her belly is full with my child. Her pussy squeezes me hard, milking me for all I've got. I drain my heavy balls inside her stomach, coming again and again until she's leaking my cum. It feels so good to breed her, to have this raw moment of undiluted bliss to share. We drift away to paradise in each other's arms, our bodies joined together in a sexual dance.

When I open my eyes, Willow's face is bright with an afterglow.

"I can't believe you're mine, Mason. My husband. I never even thought we would be here together someday." I could gaze into those dark brown eyes forever and never get bored. "I love you, husband. You're all my dreams come true. I can't wait to experience forever with you."

I hold her close, pulling out of her and collapsing on the

bed together. As my hands cup her swollen womb, I whisper in her ear. It feels great to hold my wife's naked body close, knowing she belongs to me. "I love you, Willow. You're everything I wanted and more. Being with the woman I love every day is the best kind of life. You'll always be my milky addiction."

We spend the rest of the night in bed, pursuing pleasure together. Even when the dawn breaks, I want more. It's a good thing we have the rest of our lives to indulge in this consuming, passionate love.

ABOUT THE AUTHOR

Jade Swallow is an author of super steamy novels. She loves reading and writing filthy tales featuring all kinds of kinks. Follow her on Instagram @authorjadeswallow for news about upcoming books.

Sign up for my newsletter here to get updates about my upcoming releases: subscribepage.io/eiSMM1

ALSO BY JADE SWALLOW

Want to read more books in the Dark Fantasies series?

Milkmaid for my Bully: A dark high school milking fantasy with pregnancy

My Tutor, My Stalker: A dark high school stalker romance with milking and pregnancy

Miked by my Ex's Older Brother: A forbidden age gap hucow milking fantasy with pregnancy

Love Daddy kink, breeding, and milking? Check out these books:

Breeding the Babysitter: A forbidden age gap billionaire romance with pregnancy (Forbidden Daddies #1)

Mountain Daddy's Curvy Maid : A grumpy-sunshine age gap romance with pregnancy and lactation (Mountain Daddies #1)

Pregnant by the Mafia Boss : A forbidden age gap mafia romance with pregnancy (Mafia Daddies #1)

Lessons in Love with my Brother's Best Friend: A forbidden age gap erotica with pregnancy and BBW milking

Milked by my Best Friend's Mom : An age gap lesbian erotic novella

Looking for paranormal and omegaverse erotica? Check out these books by me:

The Vampire's Milkmaid: A gothic fated mates billionaire vampire romance with breeding, milking, and pregnancy (Paranormal Mates #1)

Stranded on the Shifter's Mountain: A Fated Mates Werewolf

Shifter Romance with Breeding and Pregnancy (Paranormal Mates #2)

A Hucow Nanny for the Alpha Daddies: An age gap reverse harem fated mates omegaverse novella with pregnancy and milking (Omegaverse Daddies #1)

Alpha Daddy's Omega: An age gap pregnancy knotting and pregnant short story with arranged marriage (Omegaverse Daddies #2)

The Sea God's Fertile Bride : An age gap tentacle monster erotica (Married and Pregnant Monster Shorts #1)

Beauty and the Orc: An age gap orc daddy monster romance (Married and Pregnant Monster Shorts #2)

Short story bundles with milking, age gap, and breeding:

Summer Heat Series Bundle (Summer Heat #1-5)

Feeding Fantasies Box Set (Feeding Fantasies 1-5 + 2 bonus shorts)

Creamy and Pregnant Short Stories (Billionaires & Hucows #1-5)

Creamy Fantasies Box Set (Creamy Fantasies #1-5)

Looking for more dark and steamy college-age romances by me? Check out this one:

Broken (Twisted Souls #1)

She's a serial killer on a mission, and he's her next target. But things get complicated when she begins falling for him.